**"Hot, isn't it?" Heather said. "I brought food." She pulled out two sandwiches and passed one to T.J.**

He caught her hand rather than the sandwich. "Your fingers are trembling."

Couldn't he just have let it pass without comment? But T.J. had never been one to let anything go. Throughout their school years he'd teased her mercilessly about her red hair and freckles. And she'd never made a secret about the fact that she despised him for it.

That didn't stop them from sleeping together, though. No denying the sexual pull between them, much as she wanted to. Even now she felt it, despite the other, weightier, issue on her mind.

"You're probably wondering why I asked you to meet me here."

T.J. didn't say anything. Somehow that made it even harder. She'd had a whole speech planned out. But in the end, she managed only two short sentences.

"I'm pregnant, T.J. Just thought you should know."

Dear Reader,

Have you ever known someone who seemed like such a terrific person, but who never had anything go right for her? That's what Heather Sweeney's love life has been like—up until now.

If you've read a previous book of mine, *Small-Town Girl*, you already know the history....

Heather was jilted by her first love, Russell Matthew, and she's never really gotten over that disappointment. Her subsequent marriage to a cop ended when he was shot in the line of duty. After all that, not even Heather's best friend, Adrienne, could blame her for being cynical about her chances for a happy-ever-after marriage.

But in this book, Heather finally gets her chance. For true love, a husband, a baby...the whole package.

I am always happy to hear from readers. Please contact me through my Web site at www.cjcarmichael.com. Or send mail to the following address: #1754 - 246 Stewart Green S.W., Calgary, Alberta, Canada T3H 3C8.

Sincerely,

C.J. *Carmichael*

# For a Baby

## C.J. Carmichael

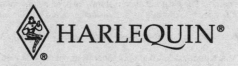

TORONTO • NEW YORK • LONDON
AMSTERDAM • PARIS • SYDNEY • HAMBURG
STOCKHOLM • ATHENS • TOKYO • MILAN • MADRID
PRAGUE • WARSAW • BUDAPEST • AUCKLAND

ISBN 0-373-71203-0

FOR A BABY

www.eHarlequin.com

**Printed in U.S.A.**

This book is dedicated to the memory of my grandma Dora,
who used to spin the most wonderful yarns.

## Books by C.J. Carmichael

**HARLEQUIN SUPERROMANCE**

851—JESSIE'S FATHER
891—HER BEST FRIEND'S BABY
917—THE FOURTH CHILD
956—A DAUGHTER'S PLACE
968—A SISTER WOULD KNOW
1038—A SECOND-CHANCE PROPOSAL
1044—A CONVENIENT PROPOSAL
1050—A LASTING PROPOSAL
1095—TOGETHER BY CHRISTMAS
1120—SMALL-TOWN GIRL
1170—LEAVING ENCHANTMENT

Don't miss any of our special offers. Write to us at the
following address for information on our newest releases.

Harlequin Reader Service
U.S.: 3010 Walden Ave., P.O. Box 1325, Buffalo, NY 14269
Canadian: P.O. Box 609, Fort Erie, Ont. L2A 5X3

# CHAPTER ONE

*Mid-April*

SHE'D MADE A MISTAKE COMING to the bar. This place wasn't going to cheer her up. She didn't even feel like drinking.

Heather Sweeney eyed the glass of vodka and orange juice in her hand and wondered how her life had come to this point. She was too young to feel washed up, but that was exactly how she felt. She was a thirty-five-year-old, widowed schoolteacher who loved children but would probably never have any of her own.

Not based on the current state of her love life. Or the state of her uterus, either, according to her doctor. She couldn't claim to be surprised by the results of the ultrasound they'd discussed at her appointment yesterday afternoon. In her family women tended to develop uterine fibroids at an early age, which was why she'd ended up an only child even though both her parents—like her—adored children.

So far, the noncancerous growths in her uterus were small enough that she could probably carry a baby to term if she were to become pregnant soon. But there was precious little opportunity for that to happen. She hadn't even gone on a date for about four months.

And while the small-town bar was almost full tonight, there wasn't a potential husband in the lot. A few middle-aged women were crowded around the video gambling machines in the back, while a gang of young men—probably barely drinking age—played pool at the other end of the room. All the tables in between were full of the farmers and miners who lived in and around this town. Most had either a wife or a girlfriend with them. Several she recognized as parents of either current or past students.

Not a decent-looking, single guy to be found.

Heather tilted her glass, watched the liquid slide over the bobbing ice cubes. Why had she come here?

She'd had other options for her Saturday night. Her best friend, Adrienne Jenson, had invited her to watch a movie with her family tonight. But it was too soon after her depressing appointment with the doctor to see Adrienne's three little boys—three!—laughing and playing and tumbling around.

She could have opted to spend the evening with her parents. But they usually played cards with the Thomsons on Saturday nights. Five was definitely a crowd when it came to bridge.

And so, because she couldn't stand to spend the night alone at her house, because there was no place else open on a Saturday night in Chatsworth, Saskatchewan, she'd ended up here. At the town bar. Alone.

The door opened, and she swung around on her stool in time to see Libby and Gibson Browning stroll in holding hands. The couple looked ridiculously young to be the parents of four kids—two girls from previous relationships and two little boys of their own. Their girls, Allie and Nicole, would be in Heather's class this year. The couple stopped to say hi to her before joining a table of their other friends.

*I'm going to finish this drink, then head home,* she promised herself. She lifted the glass to her mouth and took several long gulps. One more swallow would have done it. But she lingered just a few seconds too long. Trenton McGuire, the town lech and drunk, sauntered into the bar and headed her way.

The stool next to hers was empty, and of course that's where Trenton sat. By smell alone she could tell that whatever he ordered would not be his first of the evening.

Trenton wasn't a bad guy. When sober, he was quiet and shy, and he did manage to eke out a living on the half section of land his father had left him. But when he was drinking, he imagined himself quite a ladies' man.

"Must be my lucky night. Sittin' next to a pretty little redhead."

*Yeah, it was his lucky night, all right. Definitely not hers.* She finished her drink. Set down the glass.

"Can I buy you another, miss?"

He touched her arm and she pulled away, averting her gaze. Thank heavens he didn't seem to know her name. They'd never met, but you could never tell in a small town, who had heard of whom. "Actually, I was just leaving. Thanks for the offer, though."

She glanced at him then and felt a stab of pity. Greasy hair, poor teeth, bad skin. The man was skinny and his fingernails were dirty. Good grooming was all it would take to make him presentable. Hadn't his mother taught him anything?

"But the night is young." He put his hand back on her arm, this time holding tight. "Jerry," he signaled the bartender. "Bring her another, and a draft for me."

Though the grip on her arm was unrelenting, Heather wasn't afraid. She was in a public place, surrounded by neighbors who had known her for most of her life. "I'm sorry, but I really am tired."

She attempted again to pull away, but Trenton only moved in closer. She smelled his foul breath and tried not to grimace.

"Come on, sweetheart."

The door opened again, only this time Heather couldn't turn to see who was coming or going. Trenton had her pinned tight, his body blocking most of her view.

"Trenton," the bartender said, "I think the lady wants to go home. You'd better let go of her arm."

Yeah, because it was starting to hurt.

"But we ain't had a chance to get to know each other yet."

Heather had decided it was time to forget about the poor guy's feelings and go for a knee in his groin, when a hand clamped down on Trenton's shoulder.

"Sorry I'm late, honey. Been waiting long?"

She glanced up at a man who was about as different from Trenton as a man could be. Tall and strong, good-looking with thick dark hair and perfect teeth. And he didn't smell bad, either.

"Hey there, T.J." She'd known him all her life. Been in the same classroom from grades one through twelve. That didn't mean she felt relieved at having him ease her out of this sticky situation. In some ways T.J. posed more of a risk to her than Trenton McGuire ever could.

Trenton's hand dropped from her arm. He slunk back onto his bar stool, with a slightly fearful aspect, as if he was worried he was about to get hit. But once he'd backed off, T.J. didn't even glance in his direction again.

"Ready to go home?" he offered her his arm and after a slight pause, she took it.

People had been watching the drama with interest, a few of the men on the ready in case she really did need help. But T.J. had beaten all the wanna-beheroes to the punch. Now they returned to their drinks and conversations, not paying much attention as Heather walked with T.J. out into the evening.

She breathed deeply, taking in the fresh bite of spring air with pleasure. In the pale moonlight, the white grain elevator across the street seemed to glow. She felt T.J.'s hold tighten and shivered.

"Thanks for helping me out in there."

"You okay?"

There wasn't quite enough light for her to read his expression. She unlinked her arm and took a step backward.

"Sure. You go on ahead. Don't let me interrupt your plans." He must have been going to the bar for a reason. Maybe he was meeting someone.

"I'll walk you home." He moved toward her and offered his arm again.

She wanted to say no, yet couldn't find her voice. T. J. Collins had been back in Chatsworth for a few years now. He'd left his high-powered law partnership in Calgary to take over the Handy Hardware from his father. In all that time, she'd barely spoken to him. Despite their history, maybe because of their history, the man made her way too uncomfortable.

He started walking, taking her with him. Their strides matched, and they moved in silence, something Heather couldn't imagine doing with anyone else. Normally she tended to be a chatty person, but small talk had never worked to her advantage with T.J.

Unfortunately the lack of conversation only made her more aware of his physical presence. Of the breadth of his shoulders, the lightness of his stride and the warmth of his arm against hers.

Though he'd never been to visit, he knew which house was hers—a two-bedroom bungalow in the middle of quiet, residential Mallard Avenue.

He waited for her to unlock the door.

"Thanks again, T.J." She knew she should draw back once the words were out, but she let his gaze trap her. They stood, in the dark, on her landing, the scent of sweet lilac from the shrubs on either side of them clouding her senses.

He didn't say a word to her. Not a word. Just reached for her. And suddenly they were kissing with the instincts of lovers who knew each other very well.

Somehow T.J. ended up in her foyer, the front door closed. Heather's mind felt numb, her body wondrously alive. T.J.'s mouth was warm, incessant, gentle and demanding all at the same time. He kissed her as if he thought he might never be able to kiss another woman. All his energy, thought and desire, focused on her.

And she melted under his touch. As she always had.

"Heather."

That was all he had to say. She let him pull her sweater from her shoulders, her T-shirt over her head. He carried her to the bedroom—picked the guest room by mistake, but it didn't matter. There was a bed in here, too. They sat on the edge of the mattress, kissing again as his hands worked the clasp at the back of her bra.

Her breasts yearned to be touched. Her entire body yearned to be touched. Heat pooled in her core as she waited for his hands to make her feel all the delicious sensations she remembered clearly from their two previous encounters.

Much as she'd loved the other men in her life—Russell, her best friend and first lover; Nick, the brave police officer who'd been her husband—no one had ever made her feel quite the way T.J. did.

Wildly, crazily, brazenly woman.

He choked out another word. "Beautiful." Then bent to kiss her nipples, his hands trailing down her back, then up again, coming round her rib cage to enclose the weight of her breasts.

Making love with T.J. seemed to happen so naturally, that later Heather couldn't really identify any point in time when she'd decided, *This is going to happen.* It just did, as if it had been preordained. And maybe it had been—from that instant when he'd taken her arm in the bar.

*This is why I've tried so hard to avoid you,* she thought when they were both, finally, naked on the bed. The chemistry between them was so strong—and so inexplicable. It wasn't as if they even liked each other. When they were kids he'd loved to tease and torment her. And that hadn't changed once they were adults. So why did they keep ending up in bed together?

She knew it was wrong. She wasn't the kind of woman who slept with a man she didn't love. And yet, as T.J. rose above her, his well-defined chest outlined in the faint light from the unshuttered window, she felt as if she'd rather die than deny herself the next few hours. She put her hands to his pecs and felt the hard muscles tense. She hated to admit how much she wanted him right now.

"Heather." This time there was a question in the way he said her name.

She looked at his face. He was so focused on her, his mouth serious, his gaze steady.

"I haven't…been with a woman since my wife left. I don't have any protection with me."

She couldn't believe they'd come this far and she hadn't even thought about birth control. That was also so very not like her. She'd learned the hard way. One moment of carelessness was all it took.

But what if something *did* happen? Would it be that terrible this time? She was an adult now. In fact, this could be her last chance.

"Heather?

Their bodies were both primed for this moment.

Yet Heather knew he would stop if she told him to. What should she do? Besides her aching sexual desire, she felt another secret yearning, equally strong.

She studied the face of the man she'd known all her life. She saw an innocence in his eyes that was usually masked. She saw longing and lust. And something more. Something she'd seen before but been afraid to acknowledge.

*Tell him the truth, Heather.* She hadn't been on the pill for years.

"Make love to me, T.J. Please."

She had no idea a tear had formed in the corner of her eye until T.J. brushed it away with the tip of his finger. Then he kissed the spot tenderly.

"With pleasure," he said.

And that's exactly how it was.

## CHAPTER TWO

*Mid-June*

HEATHER AND HER BEST FRIEND Adrienne were seated at the outdoor patio of a restaurant in Yorkton. They'd finished lunch and were lingering over iced lattes. The day was sunny and warm, not too hot. Adrienne looked younger than her thirty-two years in her tank top and capris. Her fingers and toes were painted matching shades of a color that reminded Heather of grape jelly.

Finally Adrienne, who'd been amazingly patient so far, leaned across the table. "So what did you want to talk about? Come on—I'm dying of curiosity."

Heather had been waiting for the right moment. Now she realized it was never going to come. She cleared her throat. "You're the first person to hear this—"

"Oh, you've got a new boyfriend, don't you?" Adrienne grinned with excitement. "I thought you've had a certain glow lately. He's good in bed, isn't he? I just—"

"No, Adrienne. This isn't about a guy."

"Really?" Momentarily crushed, Adrienne brightened again. "I know! You've decided to take that trip to Europe. You want me to watch your house while you're gone."

"No. Not a trip to Europe. Not a trip to anywhere. Adrienne, I think...actually, I know...I'm pregnant."

Silence. Adrienne's mouth formed a perfectly round shape. She blinked her eyes once, then a bunch of times, as if she needed to clear her sight.

"But...but you haven't gone on a date in months." Her forehead creased. "How pregnant are you?"

Heather knew what she meant. "Eight weeks."

"Oh. My. God." She planted both hands on the table, then leaned back. The corners of her mouth turned up. The smile widened into something that looked a lot like delight. "You're pregnant!"

Relief flooded Heather, making her realize how much she'd been counting on her friend to have a positive reaction. Adrienne knew about her health issues. Knew, too, how giving up her and Russ's baby when she was younger still tore at her. She touched her hand to her flat tummy. Hard to believe, but the tests had confirmed the news on three separate occasions.

She was going to have a baby.

"And the father...?"

"That's the tricky part." She couldn't meet her friend's gaze for this. "It's T. J. Collins."

"T.J.?" Adrienne fell back in her chair, shocked. Then she leaned forward again and whispered, "But you don't even like him!"

"I know."

"He used to make you miserable. You'd walk an extra four blocks to school to avoid crossing his path. And I've noticed how you've gone out of your way to steer clear of the hardware store ever since he moved back from Calgary."

"I know, I know. It's totally crazy."

"On the other hand...the guy's rich, he lives in the small town you've always sworn you'll never leave and he's a hunk. I never told you this, 'cause I didn't think you'd understand, but if I wasn't married..."

"Please. I can't even *imagine* you not being married." Adrienne and her quiet husband, Ernie, had been high school sweethearts. Just like Heather and Russell. Only they'd managed the happily-ever-after part, too.

"So tell me how it happened...between you and T.J.?"

"You won't believe this. It is such a cliché." Heather explained how T.J. rescued her from the unwelcome advances of Trenton McGuire, then walked her home. "One thing just led to another and the next thing I knew, he was asking if he needed to wear protection.''

Adrienne's eyes widened. ''What did you say?''

''I didn't exactly answer his question. But I think he may have assumed from…my actions…that I had things covered.''

''Heather!''

''Yeah.'' Heather sank deeply into her chair. ''He's going to be so angry with me. Hell, *I'm* angry with me. I don't know what I was thinking. I'm a grade-four schoolteacher in a small town. I can't have a baby without being in a committed relationship.''

''Was he good, Heather? I'm guessing he was really, really good.''

She couldn't stop herself from blushing. She didn't say a thing, just sat there turning more and more red-faced.

''Really? That good? Well, no wonder you lost your head.''

''I knew I was taking a spin at Russian Roulette, but I figured, *what are the odds?*''

''And you got lucky.''

''Or not lucky.''

''Come on, Heather. You always wanted to have a kid. This is your chance.''

''Yes, but I wanted the whole package. You know, the guy and the marriage and *then* the baby.'' She frowned. ''Some days I feel so excited and thrilled about the idea of finally having another baby. But when I try to imagine going back to school, growing big and heavy under the watchful eye of all those impressionable nine-and ten-year-olds, I just don't think I can do it."

"The school board won't fire you. They can't."

"I know. But that's not the point. I don't want to be a bad role model for my kids."

"You haven't told your parents?"

Sigh. "No."

"Heather…"

"I know. I have to do it soon, but I am so dreading the conversation. Can you imagine how disappointed they'll be? My second pregnancy out of wedlock."

Even saying it now, Heather could hardly believe it. She had no idea how her life had turned out this way. She'd always been a responsible person, and she'd tried to make smart decisions with her life. She'd earned her own way through university and had many good friends and a great relationship with her parents.

But she'd been unlucky in love. First, with Russell. They'd been best of friends for years, lovers for a short while, and then he'd met Julie and everything had changed. But while he'd made a life without her, Heather had trouble forgetting about him. Easygoing Russell with his charm and intelligence and kindness had remained her ideal for many years.

She hadn't even been able to be angry with him

about their baby. She hadn't told him she was pregnant, so she couldn't blame him for doing nothing. It had taken her years to get over her own pain, however. Finally she'd married a bright, ambitious young cop from Yorkton and looked forward to a future of teaching and raising a family of her own.

But Nick had been shot on the highway when he'd stopped what he'd thought was an impaired driver. The man had been drinking all right. Unfortunately he also had a gun and was intent on committing suicide. He'd taken Nick with him.

And left Heather on her own. She'd sworn to keep clear of men after that, but loneliness had eventually compelled her to start dating again. No one really appealed for more than a couple of dates, though. And she'd begun to despair of ever having the one thing she really wanted.

A child.

"Sometimes I wonder where I made my first mistake. Was it not telling Russell I was pregnant as soon as I found out? Marrying Nick? Sleeping with T.J.?" She shook her head. "Maybe I'm kidding myself, but I really feel too smart to be this stupid."

"You've had bad luck with men."

"People make their own luck."

"Whose side are you on?" Adrienne sounded exasperated. "Is it your fault Russell fell in love with the elegant Julie? Or that Nick pulled over a crazy drunk and got himself shot? And don't you dare blame yourself for sleeping with T.J. Though, maybe, you might have been a little more honest…"

Heather felt like sinking under the table. "Oh, God, he's going to be so, so furious. Unless… Maybe I shouldn't tell him."

"Oh, right. Smart idea, Heather. And what happened the last time you got pregnant and didn't tell the guy who was responsible? Besides, maybe there's a silver lining to all this. In fact…" Adrienne stared across the street at the Co-op Grocery Store, but Heather could tell she wasn't checking out the special on frozen lemonade.

"What, Adrienne? What are you thinking?"

"I've just had the best idea." She straightened in her chair and smiled. "This is so perfect, so simple, I can't believe I didn't think of it right away."

Heather waited.

"Okay. You want to keep this baby, right?"

"Of course."

"And you don't want to be a single parent."

"Right."

"That means you need to get married."

"Brilliant, Adrienne. Why didn't I think of that?" Heather put her head into her hands. This was hopeless. The whole situation was hopeless.

"So," Adrienne carried on, "that means you and T.J. have to get married."

"Me and T.J.?"

"Yup."

"That's your perfect idea?"

"Even aside from the fact that he's the father of your baby—which is, by the way, a good reason on its own—the guy is ideally suited to you."

"T.J. is moody, unsociable and downright rude. Which of those stellar qualities makes him perfect for me?"

"He's completely different from Russell, that's what."

"Adrienne, you're not making any sense."

"Russell has been your ideal for too long. You've judged every one of your boyfriends against the standard he set. Even Nick."

Yes, it was true. She couldn't deny it.

"What you need is a man who is Russell's exact opposite. That way you won't be able to compare—they'll be too different."

"I see." Adrienne's logic was twisted, but it could be followed if you tried hard enough. "And that's why you think T.J. is so right for me? Because he doesn't have any of the qualities I admire in a man?"

"Exactly."

"I think having three sons has scrambled your brains."

"You could be right," Adrienne said cheerfully. "Tell you what. Why don't you come up with a better plan?"

*July*

HEATHER STOPPED HER MOUNTAIN bike a couple of houses back from the construction site for the Matthews' new house. They were pouring the foundation today. Heather put a hand to her forehead and squinted against the scorching summer sun.

Russell Matthew and his son stood listening to the contractor they'd hired from Yorkton. Eleven-year-old Ben, who'd been in her fourth-grade class two years ago, had shot up another couple of inches this summer. She couldn't believe how he'd grown.

The noise of the cement mixer ground out all other sounds in the hot, still air. That morning's forecast projected the mid-July heat wave to linger into the next week, too. Though it was only noon, and she was dressed in denim shorts and a pink tank top, Heather already felt uncomfortably warm. The guys had to be cooking working around all that hot cement.

No sooner did she have that thought, than a Volvo station wagon drove up. Russell's wife, Julie, stuck her head out the open driver's side window.

"Anybody thirsty?"

Russell straightened, showing off his tanned shoulders and broad chest. He and the contractor were working in jeans only. Removing his cap, he wiped sweat off his brow as he smiled at his wife. "Aren't you a sight for sore eyes."

"Hang on, I've got cold cans of lemonade and iced tea." Julie switched off the ignition, then went around to the back where she removed Emma from her car seat. The little girl wasn't yet one, but already Heather could tell she was going to be tall and honey-haired like her mother.

"Want to help Mommy take drinks to Daddy and Ben?"

Seeing the toddler hold out her trusting arms to her mother, Heather had to look away. For years she'd wanted everything that Julie had. And now. Well, now.

She glanced down at her stomach which was still flat but wouldn't be for long. She sighed, then remounted her bike and continued along Lakeshore Drive. The entire Matthew family called out greetings as she came into view, but she just smiled, waved her hand and kept on pedaling.

Much to Julie's relief, Heather was sure. Russell's wife was always polite, but too much history existed between Heather and Russ for the three of them to be real friends.

So Heather tended to avoid the Matthews as much as possible, which was hard in a small community like Chatsworth. Especially since she and Russ both taught at the local elementary school.

But it was summer break, and she had another problem on her mind today.

As Heather pedaled faster, a light breeze off the lake fingered her loose hair and sent cool shivers down her bare arms. Once she'd crossed the railway tracks, she turned left onto Willow Road. Gravel crunched under the thick tires of her mountain bike. A couple of red-winged blackbirds swooped over-head, then settled in the tall reeds growing on the swampy side of the lake. The narrow lane traced the western shoreline all the way to the public parking lot next to the concession stand.

Here she left her bike in one of the metal stands provided for that purpose, not bothering to lock it up. She unfastened her saddlebag with the lunch she'd packed that morning, and set out for the far end of the beach. On her way, she passed several groups of mothers and children spread out on blankets and wet towels along with a multitude of snacks and water toys.

Once she'd left the general beach area, she came across a pair of young lovers, partially hidden behind a clump of dark-leaved shrubs. The girl in a red bi-kini, the boy in baggy shorts riding low on his hips, were sprawled on an old blanket. The girl smoothed lotion into the young man's back with long, lingering strokes.

"Hi, Karen. Ryan."

"Oh. Miss Sweeney. I didn't see you coming."

"Sorry. I didn't mean to startle you." Hard to be-lieve these eighteen-year-olds were former pupils of hers. She remembered them both being top students. Ryan was very competitive—about school, sports, everything. Karen's sweet disposition made her a favorite of everyone's. Including Heather.

"Enjoying the summer holidays?" Ryan lifted his head and gave her a sleepy, charming grin.

"I am. Looks like you are, too."

"We don't get many days off to relax like this. Ryan's on shift work at the mine," Karen explained. Many of the locals worked at the potash mines in nearby Esterhazy. "And my mom isn't on duty at the nursing home today. Otherwise I'd be baby-sitting my brothers."

The twins would be in Heather's class this year, too. She'd heard they were a handful and hoped she was up for the challenge. She regarded the pretty young girl with sympathy. "Well, enjoy the rest of the day, you two."

She turned and breathed deeply as she continued on her way. The air always smelled different close to the lake. She was almost to the line of evergreens that separated the public beach from a privately owned golf course bordering the other side of the lake, when she finally saw him.

T.J. rested his back against the trunk of an old poplar. His dark hair was in its usual state of disarray, and the lower portion of his tanned face was covered in a light beard. He had on sunglasses, so she couldn't tell for sure, but he seemed to be watching her approach. She swallowed and forced her chin up an inch. At that moment she realized she'd been clinging to a hope that he wouldn't show up.

She glanced at her watch. Despite all the interruptions, she was here on time.

"Hot, isn't it?" She sat about three feet from him, wishing she'd thought to pack a blanket. The grass half tickled, half scratched her bare legs.

T.J. removed his sunglasses. For a second their glances snagged against each other. Then he pulled off his white T-shirt and spread it over the grass a little closer to himself. "Sit here. You'll be more comfortable."

She couldn't really say no, even though she'd have been more at ease if he had kept his shirt on. Not that long ago she'd rested her head on his muscular chest. Now, she deliberately averted her gaze from it.

"I brought food." Settled on his T-shirt—was it her imagination, or could she feel his heat burning right through to her skin?—she unzipped the insulated bag in which she'd packed their lunch. She pulled out two sandwiches, slices of cheese, a container of strawberries. She unwrapped the first tuna on sourdough and passed it to T.J.

He caught her hand rather than the sandwich. "Your fingers are trembling."

She lowered her head. Couldn't he have just let it pass without comment? But T.J. had never been one to let anything go. Throughout their school years he'd teased her mercilessly about her red hair and freckles. And she'd never made a secret about the fact that she despised him for it.

That didn't stop them from having slept together, though. The first time happened just after they graduated high school. Russ, two years older, had already left for fall term at university and there'd been no promises binding her—much as she'd wished otherwise.

The second time she and T.J. got together was in Saskatoon, where she'd been taking a break from working on her education degree to have Russ's baby. And then there'd been this April…

No denying the sexual pull between them, much as she wanted to. Even now she felt it, despite the other, weightier, issue on her mind.

"You're probably wondering why I asked you to meet me here."

T.J. didn't say anything. Somehow, that made it even harder. She'd had a whole speech planned out. But in the end, she only managed two short sentences.

"I'm pregnant, T.J. Just thought you should know."

# CHAPTER THREE

T.J. TENDED TO REACT to shocking news with silence. When his ex-wife, Lynn, had told him she was leaving, that she'd found someone new, someone who loved her, someone who didn't work seven days a week, twelve hours a day, he'd just sat in his armchair and stared at her.

The way he was now staring at Heather. He noticed small things about her. The pattern of freckles across her nose. The way the sun turned her hair to liquid copper. The slight wobble of her lips as she waited for him to speak.

He didn't know what to say. Didn't even know what he was feeling. But it was something, all right. His stomach was so tight he didn't think he could swallow a mouthful of water. The sensation felt very strange and unfamiliar.

T.J. wasn't used to feeling. For the past few years since he'd left his legal practice in the city and come home to Chatsworth to look after his father's hardware business, he'd existed in a perpetual state of numbness. But apparently no longer.

In the distance he heard the happy cries of children

playing, the buzz from the motor boat pulling a waterskier. Closer, he could hear the heavy sound of Heather breathing.

He had to say something. Had to react. But she couldn't be pregnant.

"You weren't on the pill?" He had relived their evening together about a dozen times. In his mind he always glossed over the part where he'd told her he didn't have any condoms. He couldn't remember what she'd said in response, only that there'd been a tear in her eye when she'd asked him to make love to her, and no way could he have held back after that.

She gazed down at her hands. Her small, golden, freckled hands, upon which she wore no jewelry other than her sports watch. No rings.

"I know I implied that I was on birth control, T.J. But I wasn't."

He almost smiled, as a blush revealed Heather's embarrassment. That was something else he'd always liked about her, even though she probably wouldn't guess it from the way he'd teased her.

Teasing Heather Sweeney had become habit for him during their school years. In truth, taunting her had been the only way he could get her to notice him. From a very young age, Heather had time for only one guy at school, and that was Russell Matthew, two years her senior and a virtual god in her eyes.

From what he'd observed from a distance, T.J. suspected she still carried a secret torch for the man. Given that Russ was happily married with two kids, that wasn't a recipe for Heather's future happiness. Ten years ago he could have happily offered her a solution to her dilemma. But since what had happened with Lynn—and his daughter—he didn't have much left to offer any woman. Or child.

"I have a confession, T.J. The reason I let you assume everything was okay was that I didn't care whether I became pregnant. In fact, a part of me actually hoped it would happen."

Silently T.J. turned over this new information in his mind. Heather was thirty-five years old. Widowed, with no serious boyfriend in her life. Why would she *want* to get pregnant?

"I don't get it."

Her sigh sounded long-suffering. "There was a reason I was in the bar by myself that night. It's not something I normally do. But I'd just had an appointment with my doctor."

He wanted to tell her to stop. If she had a fatal disease he couldn't stand to hear. Not Heather. But of course he didn't say anything, and she kept talking.

"The women in my family are susceptible to a certain type of problem—I'll spare you the details. But the problem can lead to early infertility. I'd had an ultrasound and the doctors told me that it was happening to me, too. I can still have a baby now, but in the future it may be a little more tricky.''

She was throwing a lot at him. And he was starting to feel angry. ''Are you saying you used me to get pregnant?''

''I suppose in a way I did.''

She sounded utterly unhappy, but he no longer cared how Heather Sweeney felt.

''Didn't you think I should have a say in whether or not I wanted to bring another child into this world?''

And his say would have been no. He'd already proven what an unfit parent he made. He'd neglected Sally, even worse than he'd neglected Lynn. He'd lost them both and he knew he had no one to blame but himself.

''It wasn't like I *planned* for it to happen. I didn't know you'd be in the bar that night, or that you'd…come home with me,'' she finished miserably. With one hand she plucked at the grass in front of her. ''I'm not proud of what I did, T.J. Not the sleeping together part. And not the birth control part, either. I guess you have every right to be angry with me.''

''Oh, hell.'' He leaned back using his arms for support and stared out at the lake. The water was silver-blue in the high afternoon sun. At the far end, he could just make out the assorted buildings and trees of Chatsworth.

"You're sure you're pregnant?"

"Three months."

"Oh, hell," he said again. Yeah, it had been about that long since he'd held her small, curvy body close to his own. During those hours they'd been together, he'd almost felt alive again. He'd almost held out hope for his future.

But she'd woken him at four in the morning. "T.J., you have to get out of here. Mrs. Manley across the street wakes up very early."

Her shoving him out the back door of her house had been more effective than a Dear John letter ever could have been, letting him know that she considered their latest encounter just another one-night stand. Each time it had happened between them, she'd reacted the same way.

Except, this time, she'd actually gotten something she'd wanted from him. A baby.

"You should have told me," he muttered again.

"I know. I'm sorry."

Finally she raised her head and let him see her remorseful expression. Then, she turned to the lake, and they sat there, side by side, together, yet alone with their individual thoughts, for many long minutes.

T.J. couldn't stop himself from reflecting over the past. This wasn't Heather's first pregnancy. The summer after her freshman year at university, she and Russell had both been back in Chatsworth working to save money for the next year at school. T.J. had been home, too, for the same reason.

Not that Heather would have noticed. As usual, she'd been totally focused on Russell. Even though they'd broken up, they'd had a brief fling that summer. At the end of it, Russ had returned to university in Vancouver, and Heather hadn't heard from him again. He'd met Julie that fall. And apparently hadn't given Heather a second thought.

T.J. didn't know when Heather had figured out she was pregnant. They'd been back at school in Saskatoon for several months before he'd noticed she wasn't hanging out around campus anymore. With some effort, he'd tracked her down to a small apartment on the other side of the river. She was working at a Dairy Queen and spending her free time reading. Alone.

He'd pretended running into her was an accident. And he'd promised he'd keep her secret. She'd been obviously pregnant by then, and though he hadn't asked any questions, he'd figured the father was Russell. He'd made a point of being around to drive her to her doctor appointments, and help with the odd small job around her place. Even though his heart had ached for her, he'd kept up his usual battery of insults and one-liners. He'd instinctively known she'd hate for him to feel sorry for her.

One night they'd watched a movie together. It had been a sad movie, and she'd cried at the end. He'd swear that he only put his arm around her to comfort her, but within seconds they were kissing. He'd felt all the same passion and heat as he had the first time they'd made love.

Inadvertently, the reason they'd been together that time had been because of Russell, too. Heather had been brokenhearted after he'd left for Vancouver. They had an agreement to date other people. But Heather only wanted Russ.

Except for that one night, briefly, she'd wanted T.J. Until the next morning, when she made it clear she considered their encounter a mistake.

The usual pattern.

"So, what's the plan, Heather? What do you want to do?"

"Well, I'm going to keep the baby, of course," she said quickly.

He didn't know why he'd bothered to ask. She'd given up her first baby—Russell's baby—for adoption. She'd just told him she had a medical condition that might make future children impossible.

"So what do you want from me? Child support?" Money he could give. He had plenty. Lynn had refused to accept a cent after their divorce, on principle. He kept a large amount in trust for Sally, but even so, he was wealthy by small-town Saskatchewan standards.

When Heather didn't answer, he turned to look at her. She met his gaze and wouldn't let it go.

"Don't tell me you want my help raising this kid, Heather. I can't do that."

"Can't? Or won't?"

"Can't. One day I'll tell you the story."

"Is this about your ex-wife and child? I heard Lynn remarried and that she's living in Toronto. What's your daughter's name?"

"Sally."

"Do you visit her?"

He wrenched his gaze away. Damn Heather. She had no business prying, and he wasn't going to answer any more of her nosy questions.

"I'm a lousy father, okay? Too bad you didn't know that three months ago when you picked me to roll around in bed with."

"Don't," she said sharply. "Don't talk about what happened between us that way."

"Why not? It was just a one-night stand. Right? You and me are the king and queen of the one-night stand."

"You have a gift for being cruel."

"Is that right?"

"Yet, I know at heart you're a decent person."

"Wow. Thanks for the resounding vote of confidence."

"I have to believe there's a reason we keep ending up going to bed together."

"Yeah. We both like sex."

She closed her eyes briefly. She was losing her

patience with him, yet he couldn't stop himself from goading her further.

"Redheads are hot in the sack."

"Stop it, T.J. I know what you're trying to do. And it won't work this time. I am not going to lose my temper with you."

"Aw. Why not?"

"Because I think we should consider getting married."

FOR THE THIRD TIME IN AN HOUR, T.J. was stunned into silence. He looked at the tuna sandwiches on the ground between them. Neither one of them had taken a bite of the lunch Heather had packed.

The sun felt so hot on his shoulders. He should have picked a spot in the shade. Heather wasn't wearing a hat. She would burn. Taking his cap from the ground beside him, he placed it lightly on her head.

How should he react to that last statement of hers? He could tell she was on pins and needles with the waiting.

"Was that a proposal?" he finally asked.

She looked different in his cap. Younger, sportier. But still cute as ever.

"Yeah. I guess it was."

And she sounded real thrilled about it, too. "Were you listening to me earlier? I've tried the husband/

father thing and I sucked at it. Big time. You deserve better.''

If he'd thought he was going to get out of it that easy, he should have known better.

''This isn't about what I *deserve,* T.J. And it sure as hell isn't about what I want, or you want. Like it or not, this baby is yours.''

Well, he'd already made it plain he *didn't* like it.

''You should have told me the truth that night.''

''Yes, I should have. And you can go on blaming me for the rest of our lives if that makes you feel better. But that doesn't change the reality of the situation. This is our baby, T.J.'' She touched her flat stomach protectively. ''And I plan to keep it.''

''I know you do. But you don't need me to marry you to do that.''

IN FACT, SHE DID. Heather was surprised T.J. was so slow on the uptake. He'd lived in Chatsworth long enough to know this town and the people who lived here.

''I am an elementary-schoolteacher, T.J. I'm in a position of enormous trust, and carry a lot of influence over the young kids of this town. I know most of their parents wouldn't approve of the example I would set if I had this child on my own. Even I wouldn't approve…''

''Heather, people will understand. You're a good person.''

"I'd like to think so. But judging from my actions these past few months, I have to wonder." Actually, she'd expected T.J. to be angrier that she'd deceived him about her birth control. She, herself, was so ashamed. Yes, she wanted to be pregnant. But not this way.

"You're being too hard on yourself again. And underestimating the terrible power of my sexual magnetism."

Lord, T.J. could sound so arrogant at times. But she wasn't deceived. She knew he was trying to make her feel better.

"Look, Heather, I'm flattered you'd consider marrying me. I know we've had kind of a…checkered history, the two of us. But there's got to be another solution. Some other guy you know who'd make a great husband and dad."

Yeah, she knew someone like that, all right. Russell Matthew.

"I wouldn't have asked you T.J. if I thought I had other options." Oh, no. That hadn't come out sounding very nice. "This is *your* baby," she reminded him.

"You're sure?"

"T.J.!"

"Well, since I've been back in town, I've seen you with quite a few different guys."

"I may date occasionally, but I'm pretty discriminating about who I go to bed with.'' In a low tone she added, ''Present company excluded.''

T.J. started to laugh, then abruptly stopped. She supposed the cold reality of the situation was finally getting to him.

''Well, what do you say?'' she pressed. ''Don't make me ask again.''

''I'm just worried you're going to be sorry you asked the first time.'' T.J. put her sandwiches back into the saddlebag. He stood, dusting grass bits from the back of his jeans. ''I've got to be going. I have a delivery to make.''

She scrambled after him, gave him back his cap, then did her best to shake his shirt clean.

''Don't worry about a little dirt.'' He took the shirt from her hands and slipped it over his head, then replaced his sunglasses.

She couldn't help thinking what a good-looking man he was. Dark hair, blue eyes, the kind of skin that tans instantly in the sun and always looks healthy. In terms of physical appearance, T. J. Collins had much to offer their child.

Too bad he didn't have what really counted.

Commitment. Love. The willingness to put another's interests above his own.

''I should have known you'd never go for this.'' She picked up the saddlebag and heaved it over her shoulder. As she turned to walk away, though, he stopped her.

"Why don't you come to my place tonight for dinner? I'll show you something. After, you let me know if you still want me to be the daddy of your baby."

HEATHER PEDALED BACK SLOWLY along dusty Willow Road. The heat was stifling now. She wished she'd thought to take a dip in the lake before heading home. At least her meeting with T.J. was over. She'd been dreading it since the doctor's appointment three weeks ago when her pregnancy was officially confirmed.

She wasn't sure how she felt about T.J.'s reaction. That he wasn't jumping up and down at the opportunity to marry her didn't surprise her. She knew she had a way of getting on his nerves.

Yet, she couldn't deny that he had been the person to help her during the hardest period of her life. Though he'd be the last to admit it, he'd been kind and thoughtful to her during those lonely months when she was pregnant and afraid in Saskatoon. And he'd kept his promise not to tell. As far as she knew, Adrienne, T.J. and her parents were the only ones in town who knew that she'd had a child and given it up for adoption.

Well, Russell and Julie knew now, too. Two falls ago, when Russell had moved his family back to Chatsworth and she'd been faced with his presence every day at work, something inside her had cracked.

The old pain of giving up her baby had returned, until finally she'd confessed the truth.

Russ had been shocked at first, but eventually he'd come to accept what she had done. And he'd agreed with her decision not to try to track down their child. She'd picked out the parents. The father was a pediatrician, the mother was willing to stay home full-time. They were good people. Their baby would be happy.

Then Julie had become pregnant with their second child, and Russell's focus had shifted inward, toward his family once more. Heather had tried not to be resentful. Or to wonder what might have happened had she told Russ she was pregnant *before* he'd asked Julie to marry him.

Old questions. Old heartbreaks. She was sick of them. This baby inside her represented her future. She wasn't going to live in the past anymore.

She wondered how T.J. planned to convince her he wouldn't be a good marital risk. She doubted he could come up with anything to change her mind. He was pretty much her last option anyway.

## CHAPTER FOUR

AT FIVE MINUTES TO SIX, Heather left her small bungalow and walked the short distance to the Handy Hardware on Main Street. Since Julie Matthew had come to town, the central drag of Chatsworth had undergone a quiet, but impressive, transformation. Beginning with the café owned by Donna and Jim Werner, and more recently a community project to create a mural on the side of the post office, the local business fronts had been refurbished. New signs, fresh paint, a green and white awning for Lucky's grocery store and pretty wrought-iron benches on the sidewalks flanked with concrete urns spilling geraniums and alyssum were among the many changes.

The fresh look was attracting visitors, and also entrepreneurs. In the past six months alone, two new businesses had started. An energetic young woman from Yorkton, Leigh Eastbrook, had opened a small ice-cream and sweet shop next to the bank. And a middle-aged couple from Manitoba had converted an abandoned home on the other side of the hardware into Nook and Cranny, a store specializing in farm-home antiques.

Both new enterprises had employed Julie Matthew to help with the design of their stores. And Heather had to admit Julie had done a beautiful job for each of them, creating an ambiance that suited the nature of the individual businesses.

Heather bypassed the main door of the hardware—which had been ''distressed'' to appear old and full of character—and headed for the unobtrusive side door that led to the two-bedroom apartment on the top floor of the building.

T.J. had lived here ever since he'd moved back to town to look after the store for his dad. His folks had finally retired—his mother had been anxious to do some traveling in the motor home she'd convinced her husband to buy. Right now the couple were somewhere in eastern Canada. T.J. tacked their post-cards on the counter next to the cash register so that the couple's many friends and customers—including Heather's own parents—could keep track of their progress.

Heather ran up the narrow stairs. She could hear strains of a Spanish guitar recording and smell something grilling. At the landing she found the door ajar. When she tapped on the wooden frame with her knuckles, it inched open.

The living room was empty. She passed through to the kitchen and spied chopped vegetables on the counter, an open bottle of wine, two plates, but no T.J. The sliding door to the balcony at the back of the building was open.

"T.J.?"

He stood at the barbecue, grilling chicken, red peppers and onions. He wore a pair of shorts and a white T-shirt. His feet were bare and as tanned as the rest of him.

Even though she'd known him all her life, sometimes his startling good looks caught her off guard. Now they made her wonder why she'd ever thought he might be willing to marry her. If a man like T.J. wanted to get married, he'd have his choice of women.

"I brought wine." She held out the bottle. "But I see you have some open on the counter."

"I do. Would you mind pouring? I don't want these veggies to burn. The glasses are in the cupboard over the sink."

He had real crystal, she was surprised to note. She poured the rich red wine into the large glass goblets, then went back out to the balcony. Space was tight, especially with the barbecue and a small wrought-iron table and two chairs. She decided to sit in one of them.

"How do you like being back in Chatsworth?" Though she loved the place, she knew small towns weren't for everyone. And T.J. had been a partner in one of the big law firms in Calgary before his divorce. It wasn't like the guy didn't have options to running a small hardware store in a town of five hundred people, max.

"It's fine."

"Do you miss the city?"

"I wouldn't know. I didn't see much of Calgary when I lived there. I traveled from home to the office and that was pretty much it."

He had to be exaggerating. "Didn't you go to the mountains—to Banff?"

"Only for conferences."

"So you don't have plans of moving back there?"

"No. Dad's already handed over the controlling shares of the business." He frowned. "Won't even let me pay for them."

"How do you feel about working in a hardware store when you have all that legal training?"

"I like the business more than I thought possible," T.J. admitted. "The strange thing is, when I was a kid I had such bitter fights with my father about this place."

Heather remembered. Many times T.J. had come to school absolutely furious with his father. On a couple of occasions he'd gotten into serious trouble when he'd tried to run away.

"What did you two fight about?"

"If you asked me fifteen years ago, I would have said everything. Now I think Dad was just so desperate for me to take over the family business that he pushed too hard. As a result, I became determined to move away and get into *anything* but the hardware business.''

"How did you ever agree to come back here?"

"It was Mom's suggestion, after my divorce. Initially I was only supposed to stay long enough for them to go on one trip."

T.J. scraped the chicken and veggies off the grill onto a chopping board, then proceeded to dice. "I don't know which of us is more surprised about the way it's ended up. Me, that I like my father's business, or my dad that he's actually enjoying driving that motor home all over the country."

"Well, he's worked hard. He deserves a break." T.J.'s parents were both in their early seventies, a little older than her own mom and dad who still ran their own farm about five miles out of town.

Finished with the chopping, T.J. carried the wooden carving board to the kitchen. Heather followed and watched as he tossed all the food into a large ceramic bowl.

"I'll let that cool a bit. It's too hot for a warm meal, don't you think?"

"Absolutely." He had an air-conditioning unit running somewhere in his apartment—probably in his bedroom. She could hear the distant hum of the motor. Still, the temperature inside was probably in the high eighties. She pressed her wineglass against the bare skin at the top of her chest, enjoying the cooling sensation.

From across the counter, T.J. watched. She felt a different kind of heat knowing he was familiar with every curve on her body. She wondered if that's what he was thinking about now, too. When their gazes met—and held—she knew he was.

"You look nice in that dress."

The words were bland. The expression in his eyes wasn't.

"Thanks." She swallowed a sip of her wine and backed up a step. He'd looked at her this way before, and she could remember only too well how those situations had ended. She hadn't come here to wind up in his bed. This time she wanted his ring on her finger.

WITH SOME EFFORT, T.J. turned from Heather and concentrated on the meal again. In the years he'd gone to university and worked in Calgary, he'd never met a woman with the particular combination of sweetness and sensuality that made her so irresistible to him.

He added slices of avocado and chunks of lettuce to the meat and veggies in the bowl, then drizzled olive oil and balsamic vinegar on top. Finally he crumbled goat cheese into the bowl and tossed everything together. "That's it."

"It looks delicious."

They went out on the balcony to eat. T.J. tried not to notice Heather's generous cleavage in her strappy pink sundress, or to remember how erotic he'd found the bra she'd been wearing the last time he'd been with her.

Unlike many redheads, Heather had a thing for pink. Even her underwear…

Oh, God. He couldn't focus when he was around her. He'd never been able to. What was it about Heather? Not just her looks, but everything about her from her soft voice to her kind, generous nature had always appealed to him.

Maybe because she was just so different from him. She always found it so easy to laugh, to praise, to offer help. Whereas he tended to be critical and caustic and reserved. No wonder Lynn had left him…

T.J. pushed aside his half-eaten meal and strode into the house. He found what he was looking for in the filing cabinet in his spare bedroom. When he returned, Heather put down her fork and looked at him anxiously.

"Finished?" he asked.

Her plate wasn't empty, but she nodded. "I guess so."

"Good." With one hand, he pushed aside her plate to make room for the file folder. "I want you to look through these photographs. Tell me what you see."

He cleared their dishes to the kitchen and took his time cleaning up from the meal. After fifteen minutes, maybe twenty, he carried the bottle of wine out to the balcony and topped up both their glasses.

"Well?" he asked, once he was back in his chair.

"These are lovely, T.J., I'm not sure what you expect me to say." She picked up one photo, of a man in his early thirties, pushing a preschool girl on a swing. "This is your daughter?"

"Sally. Yes. With her stepdad. Do you see the way she's looking at him?" Without glancing at the photograph, he could. Sally was smiling with delight, her gaze on the man who had replaced T.J. in her life.

"I see," Heather said quietly.

"About a year ago I hired a private investigator. I wanted to make sure my daughter was doing okay. Turned out she was fine. Better than fine. They make a nice family, don't you think?" He saw Heather pick up a picture of the three of them walking along the boardwalk on the edge of Lake Ontario. Sally was in the middle, gleefully skipping, while his ex-wife and her new husband smiled with delight and pride at each other.

"I suppose so, T.J., but—"

"No buts," he said, interrupting her and not caring. "Lynn and Sally were never that happy when they were living with me."

He took the file from her hands and closed it firmly. He couldn't stand to look at the photographs. Sometimes he wondered why he hadn't burned the entire portfolio the minute after he'd received it.

"When I was married to Lynn, I barely saw her. I worked twelve-hour days at the office and weekends, too. I told myself I was doing it for my family, but I really wasn't." With hindsight, he knew he'd been addicted to his job, to the rush he got whenever he closed a deal or made a client happy.

"You were trying to make a name for yourself."

Trust Heather to make excuses for him. "I was a workaholic. Whenever I was at home, I secretly wished I could be at the office. I hardly saw my daughter. I can count on one hand the number of times I changed her diaper."

Finally he saw doubt shadow Heather's eyes. "But you loved her…"

"Frankly, I'm not sure I did. I sure didn't act like it. As for my wife, I figured a diamond bracelet would do when I didn't have time to take her out for dinner to celebrate her birthday."

"T.J.!"

At last, she was hearing what he was trying to say. "I really was a lousy husband, Heather. And even worse as a father. The reason I showed you these pictures is to make you understand. You want what you see in those photos, don't you?"

Heather glanced down at the happy trio by the lake—mom, dad, child—and nodded.

"But if you marry me, you'll never get it."

# CHAPTER FIVE

*August*

"LOOK AT THAT. They're starting to frame the Matthew place." Adrienne dismounted her bike to watch.

Heather stopped, too, leaning over the handlebars and thinking she wasn't going to be able to do this much longer. Already she could only wear shorts with elasticized waistbands.

She noticed a few of the workmen stop and look in their direction. She supposed they had their eyes on Adrienne. With her dyed hair—a shade between burgundy and purple—and eccentric wardrobe, Adrienne always stood out in a crowd.

"I've seen the plans. They're going to be using cedar shingles and lots of river rock for the veranda. Arts and Crafts style, I think it's called." Adrienne read a lot of decorating magazines when business was slow at her hair salon.

"I'm sure it will look wonderful when it's finished."

"Don't all of Julie's projects?"

Was there just a hint of rancor in Adrienne's voice? Heather was glad she wasn't the only one who found the perfection of Russell's wife a little tiresome. She tilted her head to one side, watching as a shirtless Russell nailed a two-by-four into place. Surely he'd be quitting for the day soon. It was almost six o'clock on a hot, humid Sunday. She bet Russ would really enjoy a swim about now.

Down the street a few houses, his son, Ben, was kicking around a soccer ball with one of his pals. He'd probably started out helping, Heather figured. This house had been a family project from the start. Julie, an interior designer by training, had drawn the plans. Russ had brought them to work and shown the entire teaching staff: a two-story home with a large porch out front, supported by four tapered columns, two on either side of the generous doorway.

In June the original home had been razed and work started shortly thereafter. Since school had let out for the summer, Russ had worked with his contractor and his crew, his son often by his side.

"Hey there, Ms. Sweeney."

Heather waved at the boys. Of course, their calls alerted Russell to her and Adrienne's presence. She tried not to feel self-conscious when he smiled around the nail in his mouth and raised his hammer in salute.

Worried Adrienne might attempt to start a conversation, Heather gave her friend a shove at the small of her back. "Keep pedaling. Your family's going to be starving by the time we get there."

Sunday was the one day of the week when Adrienne closed her beauty salon. Her husband and kids were already across the lake at a ball game. Heather and Adrienne were supposed to meet them with a picnic dinner of fried chicken and potato salad, but those plans had been sidelined when Adrienne decided to give Heather an impromptu manicure—which Heather considered a waste of time. In twenty-four hours the polish would be chipped and she'd have broken at least one nail. But Adrienne, once her mind was fixed on something, could be difficult to dissuade. So instead of the chicken feast they'd planned, they had ham and cheese sandwiches in their saddlebags, fresh brownies and fruit.

"My family will survive another fifteen minutes." Still, Adrienne pushed off from the curb and the two friends cycled in tandem down the quiet street. They passed the kids playing soccer and were soon out of town, winding their way along graveled Willow Road.

Heather thought of the last picnic she'd had across the lake. T.J. had been avoiding her since. She didn't blame him. She still groaned whenever she thought about how she'd practically begged him to make an honest woman out of her. She'd really put her pride on the line. Talk about embarrassing.

Somehow Heather's parents had heard about her

dinner at T.J.'s apartment and been full of questions. They knew T.J., of course.

Heather had made light of the dinner, refusing to call it a date, all the while realizing that one of these days, she'd have to tell them T.J. was the father of her baby. First she'd have to tell them she was pregnant again.

As if reading her thoughts, Adrienne picked that moment to ask, "Seen anything of T.J. lately?"

Heather grunted.

"I stopped in the other day to buy a new chain for Davey's bike. If you ask me, he looked like a man with a lot on his mind."

"I'll bet."

"I still think you two should get married. In my opinion—"

"Adrienne. Give up on it already, would you?"

She sighed. "Well, you're going to have to do something. And soon. You won't be able to keep your pregnancy a secret much longer."

Heather felt her friend's eyes on her waistline. Self-conscious, she sucked in her stomach. "Am I showing?"

"Not really. Though your bust is even bigger than usual—lucky you." Adrienne had a pear-shaped body, with slim shoulders and small breasts. She'd tried every exercise program she'd ever heard of to try to redistribute her weight, to no success.

Rounding the final curve in Willow Road, they

cycled past a family pulling their motorboat out of the lake. From the baseball diamonds on the right came the distinctive hollering and cheering of a good-natured game. A small crowd was gathered on the bleachers behind the fence at home base. Heather spotted ten-year-old Davey in left field. He smacked his fist into his glove, then waved at them.

"Why don't you watch the end of the game?" Heather suggested. "I'll see if I can nab one of the picnic tables on the hill behind the concession stand." They'd have a view of the lake up there, and with all the trees, some privacy, too.

"Sounds good." Adrienne veered off the road on her mountain bike, already hollering at the umpire who'd just walked the last batter.

Heather kept pedaling past the other ball diamonds, where yet more kids were engrossed in the last innings of their games. She passed the concession stand, waving at Herb who was scooping ice cream for the twins who'd be in her class next year. Coward that she was, she snuck past the boys hoping they wouldn't waylay her. She wanted to nab that table....

The hill was steep and she eventually had to get off her bike and start pushing it up the incline. She passed a couple necking in a discreetly shaded area, and wondered if it wasn't Karen and Ryan again.

Funny how fast time went by. It didn't seem that

long ago that she and Russell were the ones making out at the lake.

But it *was* a long time ago. She had to stop letting every little thing remind her of those happy, carefree days. Maybe if she'd moved away from Chatsworth forgetting would have been easier. But Heather couldn't imagine leaving the small town where she'd grown up.

She was huffing now. At least the picnic table was free. She could see it, tucked into a clearing, surrounded by poplars. There was one other table up here, off to the right and down a little. Maybe she could grab that one, too, so that the kids and their friends—

"Oh."

T.J. was sitting on the second table, his feet planted on the bench, an open book in his hands. He was at least as surprised to see her as she was to spot him.

"Heather?"

She dropped her bike to the grass. "That's some hill."

He eyed her midriff and frowned. "Should you be doing something so strenuous?"

"I'm fine." She put a hand on her hip, wishing she didn't need to draw a breath after every word she spoke and that her T-shirt wasn't clinging to her chest with perspiration. Sunday was also the one day of the week when T.J. closed the hardware. Just her luck to find him up here.

"So what are you doing? Besides taking your bike for a stroll?"

"Looking for a picnic spot." *If you must know.* "Adrienne and her family are joining me after Davey's ball game. But I don't want to disturb you." She bent to retrieve her bike, not looking forward to having his eyes on her as she wheeled the darn thing back down the hill.

"What's wrong with that table?" He pointed to the free one she'd originally planned to stake.

"You're reading. We'll be noisy. I'll see if there are any free tables by the playground." It wouldn't be as scenic, but at least she wouldn't have to endure the scrutiny of the man who'd spurned her proposal of marriage.

Oh, why had she thought about that? She could feel the backs of her ears start to burn.

"Put the bike down, Beatrice."

Heather chafed at his use of her middle name. For some reason he'd latched onto it on her very first day of grade one when the teacher had been doing a very thorough job of roll call.

T.J. jumped to the ground and took the handlebars from her. He pushed the bike to a tree and chained it up so it wouldn't fall.

"What are you doing with my bike?"

"Don't be so damn stubborn. Take the picnic table. Take both of them. I was about to leave, anyway.''

''It didn't look like you were planning to leave.''

T.J. glanced up into the branches of a nearby tree and spoke as if to someone he saw hiding there. ''Even when I try to be nice to her, it doesn't work.''

''Your definition of nice doesn't jibe with my definition of the word.'' She thought of all the teasing she'd endured. She didn't think he'd meant to be mean. But some days she had truly dreaded being in the same classroom as him. ''It never has.''

''You've always been tough enough to take it.''

Under his observation she could almost feel her waistline and boobs expanding. She crossed her arms over her chest.

''Told anyone yet?'' he asked.

''Adrienne,'' she admitted, uncomfortably.

''Not your parents.''

Her gaze sank to the ground. ''Not yet.''

''Don't suppose you've found a prospective groom, either?''

''T.J.!'' As usual, he had to push until she snapped. ''Just leave me alone, okay?'' Out of all the single men in Chatsworth—and there were a few, if not many—why had she chosen *him* to go to bed with?

''Hey, why so touchy? Just wondering if that marriage proposal was still open. That's all.''

''Why would you care?'' The heat of embarrassment spread from her ears to her face. Trust T.J. to milk this for all it was worth.

"I've been thinking the situation over." He stood formally in front of her, arms behind his back, feet splayed.

Heather froze, confused by his change in tone. Suddenly he looked, and sounded, just like the lawyer he'd been trained to be.

"Upon some reflection," he continued, "I'd like to reconsider my reply to your offer of the other day."

It took a few seconds for what he was saying to sink in. "T.J.? Are you serious?"

"Absolutely. I think getting married is the right thing to do. If you'll still have me?"

HE'D DONE IT. Choked out the words he knew he had to say. After thinking about their situation for weeks, he'd accepted he didn't really have a choice. Heather was pregnant, with his child.

So what if the marriage didn't last more than a few years? As a married woman, Heather would retain her reputation and respectability in the small town she'd always loved. She could hold her head high when she had this baby—their baby.

As for the child, well, he or she would be legitimate under the law. If that wasn't as important in today's society as it had once been, T.J. knew it was still worthy of consideration.

"I want to give our child a name, Heather. And I can promise to be a faithful husband and a good provider. Beyond that—no guarantees. I think I've been pretty open with you about my flaws. As if you weren't already familiar enough with them."

When she didn't say anything right away, he stuck on a proviso. "Of course, if you've changed your mind and don't want to go through with marriage after all, I'll understand."

Heather's pretty face was still deeply flushed. Obviously she hadn't expected this about-face on his part. T.J. waited for her reply, not sure what he even wanted her to say.

At one time marriage to Heather would have seemed like the answer to his prayers. But his real life experience with marriage and fatherhood had taught him his shortcomings. Some people were better off alone. He was one of them.

Gradually the confusion in her eyes faded, and her gaze sharpened on him. A shallow frown line formed between her eyebrows as she contemplated him closely.

What did she see? T.J. didn't kid himself. Heather was as aware as anyone of his foibles and character flaws.

"We're talking about a real marriage, right?"

"What other kind is there?" Slowly his lips curved into a grin, as he figured out what she was really asking. "You mean will there be sex? Hell, yeah, there'll be sex. That's the one thing I know I can do right.''

Her flush deepened. ''Oh, T.J., this is so crazy.''

He had to agree there.

''But, yes, I will marry you.''

He knew she was accepting him for the baby's sake. Yet, for a moment he felt a warm glow of happiness. *Fool,* he told himself. But knowing he was didn't change a thing. He took her small hand and squeezed it, wanting to kiss her but not sure whether such a move would be appreciated. He was just stepping in close enough to make the kiss at least an option, when a voice startled him, startled them both.

''T.J.! Imagine running into you here.'' It was Adrienne, with her husband and a pack of at least five children in tow. ''Want to join us for a ham and cheese sandwich?''

# CHAPTER SIX

"Oh, honey. This is a lot to take in at once." Heather's mother shook the dirt off her hoe, then set it against the shed wall. She brushed off her hands, covered in gardening gloves, then settled them on her hips and examined her daughter's expression carefully.

"I know." Heather picked up the basket of tomatoes at her feet. Her parents ran a three-acre, U-pick garden just off the highway that connected Chatsworth to the larger center of Yorkton. In season they had strawberries, raspberries, saskatoons, tomatoes and corn.

"Let's go have something to drink." Marion Sweeney led her daughter along the cobblestone path to a gazebo Heather's father had built just last summer. A pitcher of lemonade and melting ice cubes sat on the rattan table inside. She removed her gardening gloves, then poured two glasses and handed one to Heather.

"How are you feeling, honey?" Her gaze dropped to her daughter's middle.

"Fine. Tired, I guess. But fine other than that."

She'd come by this morning with the excuse that she wanted tomatoes, but really to tell her mother her news when her father wasn't around. Heather loved her father, but the lines of communication with her mother were much more open.

Her story had flooded out in a rush of words. The pregnancy, the engagement, the wedding which was to happen in two weeks, everything, in one breath.

"Sit down. Put your feet up."

Heather did sit, but she kept her sandaled feet on the ground. "Really, I'm as healthy as can be, Mom."

Her mother had dark hair and fair skin, which she protected with a combination of sunscreen and wide-brimmed hats. She removed the pretty straw one she was wearing today and set it on the floor next to a watering can.

"The fibroids…?" she asked.

"The doctor says they're small enough at this point they shouldn't cause a problem."

"Thank goodness."

"Yes."

"What about later?"

"I'll probably have to have a hysterectomy just like you did."

After a brief pause, her mother reached across the table for her hand. "A *baby*. This is wonderful, Heather."

"I know." Her parents had suffered almost as

much as she had when she'd made the decision to put her first baby up for adoption. When she'd married Nick, they'd been so excited by the prospect of more babies. But then Nick had died. By now her parents had probably given up on grandchildren. Among their contemporaries they were the only ones without even one. Now, finally, there would be a new child in the family.

And a new son-in-law, too.

"About T.J...." Marion's warm gaze slipped a few degrees right of her daughter. "I didn't realize the two of you were dating. You said that one dinner was just between friends?"

"We've known each other all our lives," Heather pointed out.

"Yes."

Her mother frowned, probably remembering all the times Heather had come home from school steaming mad at something awful T.J. had said or done. Her mom didn't know that during the lonely term of her pregnancy in Saskatoon, T.J. had been her only friend. That was the one time in her life when she could remember him not being totally insufferable.

"I was hoping we could have the wedding here. If that's okay with you and Dad." Her mother's rosebushes, bordering the gazebo, would make a perfect backdrop for wedding photos.

"Well, of course, honey." Marion's forehead

wrinkled with concern. "You're not rushing into this because of the baby are you?"

"Actually I am." Heather couldn't see any point in being deceptive. "But isn't it a good reason? I'm going to have his baby. I'm thirty-five and so is he. Neither of us have any other prospects in our lives."

"That sounds so...clinical."

"Not clinical. Logical."

"Oh, honey. I wish—" She picked up the glass of lemonade, took a small sip, then set the glass down again.

Heather rested her hands on her belly. She could hardly wait for the day when she would feel a mound beneath her palms and experience the subtle stirrings of a new life inside of her. In fact, she looked forward to every single aspect of pregnancy. She didn't even care about labor pains or stretch marks. She wanted this child so very badly.

The sun was blazing again on this late summer afternoon. Heather could hear the buzzing of bees in the nearby flowers. A gentle breeze wafted the sweet scent of roses through the gazebo. The peaceful setting made her wish she could spend the afternoon resting in here.

But first she had to finish her conversation with her mother. She knew there was more to come. Her mother, always diplomatic, was merely weighing her words.

Finally she leaned forward in her chair. "I know

you're a grown woman, Heather, with a good mind and lots of common sense.''

She smiled, and Heather knew that her mother meant what she was saying. She knew that whatever mistakes she'd made in her life, her parents loved her. And were proud of her.

''But are you sure you've thought through this marriage idea?''

Heather leaned forward and folded her hands on the table. ''Yes.''

Frown lines deepened the grooves on either side of her mother's pretty mouth. ''T. J. Collins is well educated, and financially secure. He's a good-looking man, too, I can't argue with that. But, I've heard some stories that aren't very complimentary.''

Heather's mother was well connected to the gossip sources in town—most of them members of the local bridge club. Marion, herself, was always careful what she passed on. When she'd been a child, Heather had often been frustrated that her mother was so close-mouthed. She had to go to school to hear all the rumors that the other children heard at home.

''You know those old biddies make up half the things they talk about.''

''Now, Heather. They exaggerate at times, I'll agree. But I don't believe they actually fabricate stories.''

''Well, what did they tell you about T.J.?''

Marion topped up both glasses of lemonade,

clearly uncomfortable. "There are rumors about why he left Calgary to come back and run his father's hardware."

"He left because his marriage fell apart. His wife took their daughter and moved to Toronto."

"Yes, that's true. But some say there were problems with his business, too."

"The law firm?"

Her mother nodded. "I heard T.J. embezzled funds from the practice and was asked to leave, on threat of disbarment."

Rumors of murder couldn't have seemed more outlandish to Heather. "No way," she insisted.

"Heather." Her mother's voice carried a gentle rebuff. "You'd better make sure you know the truth before you marry this man."

HEATHER COULD NOT TAKE HER mother's warning about T.J. seriously. T.J. wasn't an embezzler. She was so certain, she didn't even ask him about it when they met the next evening to discuss wedding plans.

They both wanted to keep the event very simple. T.J.'s parents were still on the other side of the country in their motor home, so they wouldn't be able to attend.

"Mom was all for buying a plane ticket for the weekend," he said, "but I convinced her she could throw us a party later, and she seemed happy with that."

With his parents taken care of, she broached the hardest subject. "Have you invited your daughter?"

"Sally?"

She could tell it hadn't crossed T.J.'s mind that he should include her in the wedding plans.

"She might get a kick out of being a flower girl. A lot of little girls love that sort of thing."

"She's only four. And she's never been anywhere without her mother."

"Well, naturally Lynn would have to come, too."

"You expect me to invite my *ex-wife* to the wedding?" T.J. got up from her sofa and strode across the room. "No way, Heather. This is getting way out of control. You, me, your mom and dad. That's it. No one else."

"So I get no say in planning our wedding." She twisted her hands together, conscious of the fact she wore no engagement ring. She and T.J. had decided simple wedding bands would be enough.

T.J. glared. "Not if it means you're going to invite my kid and my wife."

"*Ex*-wife."

His mouth tightened. "Exactly."

Heather leaned forward, burying her hands in her thick hair. The subject of his old marriage was obviously an emotional land mine for T.J. If their marriage was going to have a shot for long-term success, he had to deal with his feelings.

"You're still so wound up about the past, T.J. Ever considered therapy?"

His dark gaze turned into laser points of quiet fury. "No. And you won't mention the idea again, either."

"Okay, then." She took a deep breath and straightened her back. She would not let him derail this discussion. She was almost four months pregnant. The new school year would be starting in one week. They were running out of time.

"No flower girl. No therapy. So where does that leave us?" She picked up the notebook she'd purchased at Lucky's two weeks ago and consulted her list. "I've booked the minister for next Sunday afternoon. You're taking care of the marriage license. And the rings."

She lifted her head to confirm this, and he nodded.

"Mom is making us a small dinner after the service, so we don't have to worry about food. I thought I'd pick up a bottle of champagne, though...?" Again, she looked up to make sure he was okay with this.

"I'll get the champagne."

"Fine. I've booked a photographer."

"Couldn't we just get the minister to snap a couple of photos?"

She bit her lip. "I suppose." He was really being a grinch about this wedding. But what could she expect? He was T.J., after all.

Was it possible her mom was right, that she was making a mistake?

Heather closed her eyes, pushed away the dangerous thought. In seven days she was getting married. She couldn't afford doubts, at least not any more than she already had.

No, T.J. wasn't perfect. But who was? Nick had been moody at times, fond of going out for drinks with the boys after his shift when she would have preferred for him to come home to her. They'd worked around the problems and found a way to be happy together.

She'd do the same with T.J. She was going to make this marriage a success. T.J. was a smart man. He could learn to be a good husband and father. Her baby would grow up in a happy home.

"Cold feet, Heather?" T.J. was leaning against the wall, his arms folded in front of him.

She got off the sofa to confront him. "They've been blocks of ice from the very beginning."

"Then why go through with it?"

"You know why."

Dangerous lights danced in his eyes as he reached out to touch the side of her face. "You're right to be worried. Don't expect me to turn into the perfect family man. I have to work a lot of late nights at the hardware. Saturdays, too."

"I know."

"I don't do diapers. Or bottles. Or baby food."

"We'll see." Though he was speaking gruffly, his hand on her face was very gentle. She didn't have the willpower to back away from him. Not even when his hand slid down to her throat, to the first button of her sleeveless top.

She swallowed. Desire made her body heavy and warm. How did he do this to her? With just the light touch of one finger, that knowing gleam in his eye. It was as if he could see the way her body responded to him.

"Don't think you're going to change me, Heather."

As he spoke, he lowered his mouth toward hers. She rose to her tiptoes, closed her eyes, aching for the moment when the two of them would connect.

When he did kiss her, she couldn't stop the moan of pleasure she gave him in response. She could tell he was glad for this power he had over her, but she didn't care. Right now, at this moment, what he was offering was all she wanted.

ON THE MORNING OF HEATHER'S wedding day, Adrienne gave her the full beauty treatment. Hair styling, pedicure, manicure and facial.

"I'll do your makeup for you, too," Adrienne offered. This was her wedding gift, which she'd insisted on giving, even though T.J. had nixed inviting her and Ernie to the ceremony.

Heather passed on the makeup. With her coloring

she didn't need much, and Adrienne could be a little heavy-handed in that area.

Actually, Adrienne could be heavy-handed in every area, but through years of conditioning she'd grown to accept that the only color Heather would allow on her nails was the palest of pinks. Heather's hair was naturally such a vibrant shade that even Adrienne had never suggested highlights. But she did have an idea for the wedding. One that Heather liked.

"How about I straighten your hair and just curl the ends under a little?"

Heather looked at her reflection. Since it was almost the end of summer, her freckles had pretty much taken over her face. From a distance, it almost looked like a tan. As for her hair, well, she'd grown accustomed to the wild orange color and unruly curls. She couldn't even imagine what she would look like with straight hair. But the idea was appealing.

"Okay, straighten the hair and do the nails and the facial, but no makeup."

"I can live with that." Adrienne led her to the sink to get started. Since it was Sunday, she had no other customers.

Heather had never felt more like a princess. At one point, her feet were in a hot water soak, her fingernails were splayed out in front of her so the polish wouldn't smear, her face was coated in a mud mask, and Adrienne was clipping her hair.

"I feel like a movie star."

Adrienne sighed. "I *love* doing weddings."

Heather felt guilty that hers was such a simple affair. "I tried to talk Mom into getting her hair done, too, but she insisted she'd rather stay home and organize the dinner. It's only going to be the four of us. I don't know why she's making it out to be such a big deal."

Or maybe her mom just didn't want to face her before the ceremony. She and T.J. had gone over for dinner last week to talk about the plans and her mom had been decidedly cool. Heather wasn't sure if T.J. had noticed. But she had.

She hoped her mom wasn't going to mope at the wedding.

"Adrienne, have you heard any rumors about T.J. and that law firm he worked for in Calgary?"

Adrienne's hands stilled. "What kind of rumors?"

Heather tried to catch her gaze in the mirror, but Adrienne suddenly seemed very focused on a certain strand of Heather's hair.

"That he was forced to leave the partnership because he was suspected of embezzling funds?"

Adrienne swallowed.

"You *have* heard the rumors."

"Well, yes, but you know the way people like to gossip around here."

Heather looked down at her hands. Her nails

were perfect ovals, gleaming with their fresh coat of polish.

"You can't believe it's true." Adrienne attacked Heather's hair with a brush, her strokes hard. "T.J. wouldn't do something like that."

"I know," Heather said softly. "That's what I told my mom."

"Just think about your baby," Adrienne advised. "Think of how happy you're going to feel in five months when you're cuddling that child in your arms."

She picked up a can of something and began to spray vigorously. Heather closed her eyes and held her breath. Adrienne was right. She had a lot to be thankful for. Why invent problems where none existed?

THE WEDDING WAS PROBABLY ONE of the more casual on record in Chatsworth, where big church affairs with a dinner and dance following at the town hall were the norm. Because it was so hot, the men wore white shirts without jackets. Heather had picked out a sundress and matching pink sandals.

Her hair did look wonderful. Both of her parents gave her copious compliments, but it was the way T.J.'s eyes glowed when he first saw her that truly made her feel beautiful.

The corn was at its peak this time of year, so they had fried chicken and corn on the cob for dinner. Her mom had prepared two salads and baked a small wedding cake. They ate in the screened gazebo, which kept the prowling wasps from spoiling their meal. T.J. opened the champagne and she allowed herself a couple of sips before switching to sparkling apple juice.

Her dad toasted their future. T.J. toasted his lovely bride. Though Heather was certain her mother still had misgivings about this union, she couldn't fault her behavior. Her mother smiled and chatted and made sure everyone had plenty to eat and drink. Only someone who knew her really, really well would have guessed that she held reservations about her new son-in-law.

Once they'd finished cake and coffee, Marion disappeared into the kitchen. She refused to allow Heather to come with her.

"I'm just going to put away the leftovers so they don't go bad. I'll only be a few minutes," she promised.

Heather relaxed in her chair and watched T.J. and her father chat. She was a little surprised at how well the two men had hit it off. Perhaps T.J. found her father's easygoing nature a welcome change from his more intense father.

She listened as they talked about grain prices and estimates for this year's crop yield. T.J. looked younger than usual, reminding her of his teenage self. He'd managed to avoid that awkward adolescent phase that rendered so many boys gangly and unattractive. She put a hand to her tummy, hoping that their child inherited the looks from the Collins' side.

T.J. chuckled at something her father said. She liked the way laughter softened the lines on his face. He had such a direct way of looking at people. That was a sign of honesty, wasn't it?

He bent over and picked up one of her mother's cats who'd somehow snuck into the gazebo. He held the creature on his lap, scratching her under her chin, on the top of her head.

Noticing that she was watching, he smiled at her. "I like cats," he said.

"So do I."

Her father knew an opportunity when he saw one. "Want one for a wedding gift?"

T.J. raised his eyebrows at her. She shook her head. "These are outdoor cats, Dad. They'd never be happy in town. You have to give us one when it's a kitten."

T.J. lifted the feline on his lap to eye level. "Sorry. Looks like it's a no-deal."

She smiled. She hadn't realized that he liked animals. That was another good sign, wasn't it?

Besides, if he truly had stolen his client's money, surely he'd have absconded to a tropical island with a leggy blonde, rather than moved to a small prairie town to take over his father's hardware store.

HEATHER AWOKE THE MORNING after her wedding feeling more than a little strange. Tangled in the covers next to her, T.J. looked utterly gorgeous. For all the occasions they'd made love, this was the first time they'd woken up together.

Heather wondered what it would be like to ease her husband into wakefulness with a playful nuzzle on the neck. She'd love to run her hands down his body right now and see how quickly she could make him respond.

But what if T.J. didn't like morning sex? They'd never made love during daylight hours, either. Suddenly she felt bashful about the very idea of it. So, instead, she slipped out from between the sheets, determined to do something else to get their married life off to a good start.

She'd make him breakfast. A big, hearty, eggs-and-bacon breakfast, with coffee and toast and maybe fruit salad, too, if the bananas hadn't gone bad.

In her housecoat, Heather puttered around the kitchen. She wasn't a gourmet or anything, but she enjoyed having someone to cook for. Usually, when it was just her, she ate granola and yogurt, or something else simple, in the morning.

While she waited for the bacon to crisp, she set the table and poured two glasses of orange juice. When she heard the water go on in the bathroom, she added eggs to the griddle, then made whole-wheat toast. By the time T.J.—clean and dressed for work—made his appearance, she had everything ready.

"Hope you're hungry." She turned from the stove, offering a smile, then quickly taking it back.

T.J. didn't look pleased. "I guess I should have told you I don't eat breakfast in the morning. I usually have coffee and a muffin at the café."

Heather glanced at the full coffeepot on the counter. She'd ground the beans fresh this morning.

"It's kind of a routine with me," he went on to say. "I meet Lucky there and Adrienne and sometimes Julie, too."

*Adrienne, you traitor. You never told me.* She knew it was silly, but she felt like crying.

"But maybe today I'll have a piece of toast."

T.J. took a slice from the stack on the table. Anticipating that he would sit down, Heather reached for the coffeepot. But he was already on his way out.

"Don't wait supper for me" were his last words before he shut the door between them.

Heather stood, in shock, in the center of her kitchen. Suddenly all the cooking smells made her feel ill. She rushed to the washroom, threw up in the toilet. Later, as she washed her face with cool, clean water at the sink, she told her reflection it wouldn't be smart to get sensitive about what had just happened.

So big breakfasts weren't his thing. They weren't hers, either.

But he could have pretended, for just one morning. And he could have kissed her goodbye. Didn't T.J. plan to put even one ounce of effort, outside of the bedroom, into this marriage of theirs?

# CHAPTER SEVEN

TO HEATHER THE BEAUTY OF the first day of school was in the little things. A golden wooden pencil, sharpened to a fine point. A new notebook, filled with blank, lined pages. The hint of fall tingeing the edges of the leaves on the row of poplar trees bordering the schoolyard.

A week after her wedding, she stood at the front of her classroom, looked over the rows of empty desks and relished the calm. Soon boys and girls would be tumbling inside, excited and renewed from their long summer holiday. They would be tanned and taller and, yes, even wiser, than they'd been just two months earlier.

For ten months these kids were going to be hers. Only not ten months this year. Her baby was due the first week of January, so she wouldn't be coming back to the classroom after Christmas.

Still, four months was long enough to establish real ties with her kids. She'd learn intimate details about them and their families. And she'd open herself to them, too. In her experience, that was the real way to connect with children. Some teachers insisted on establishing themselves as the aloof authoritarian figure, but that wasn't her style.

Heather picked up a piece of chalk. There was talk of replacing the blackboards with whiteboards and markers this year. The dust caused problems for some of the kids with asthma and allergies. But she would miss the smell and the distinctive sound of the chalk scratching against the board.

She wrote down her name. Then stood back to look. Heather Collins.

She hadn't changed her surname when she married Nick, but this time, because of the baby, she had. It felt strange, to be thirty-five years old and suddenly have a new name. *Heather Collins.* She mouthed the words, then said them out loud.

"Has a nice ring to it."

She swiveled to find Russ Matthew standing at the door to her classroom. He had on chinos and an open-necked white golf shirt and looked relaxed and happy.

"Congratulations, Heather. Or should I say Ms. Collins?" He walked into the room, holding out his hand and she went forward to meet him.

The minute their hands clasped together, she felt sure he would draw her closer for a big, friendly hug. She could see in his eyes that he wanted to. A few years ago, he wouldn't have hesitated. But now he did, finally just putting his other hand to her shoulder and giving a squeeze.

"I'm so happy for you, Heather."

"Thank you." She felt his joy and knew it was sincere. "There's something else, too. It isn't commonly known, but I'm also pregnant."

She watched him glance down at her free-flowing dress, which camouflaged the slight outward curve of her belly.

"Really? That's even more wonderful!" He took both her hands and held them tight. Looked at her with absolute delight on his face. "You'll be a terrific mother."

"I'm very excited." An awkward pause began to develop. She knew that they were both thinking of her first baby, the one she'd given up fifteen years ago. That first child would always cast a shadow between them.

Understandable in the circumstances, but still, to Heather, who'd had Russell's friendship for almost as long as she could remember, the slight rift between them left her unbearably sad, too.

She could have prevented some of this by keeping the secret to herself. It was her own fault this chasm had opened between them.

She forced herself to smile. "Oh, and thanks for the beautiful tablecloth. I'm afraid my thank-you letters are still sitting on my hallway table, waiting for stamps. It was so nice of you and Julie to think of us."

She and T.J. had been flooded with gifts after news

of their unexpected marriage had made the rounds. Heather had been touched to discover just how many people seemed to truly wish her well.

"Julie picked it out when she was in Vancouver this summer. She thought the colors would go well in your house."

"They do. It looks wonderful. So was she in Vancouver on business?" Julie freelanced for a décor magazine based out of the city.

"Partly," Russ said. "Also, she took the kids to our cottage on Saltspring. Because of the house, I couldn't get away this year."

"It's really coming along."

"I'm doing a lot of the work myself, which has slowed the process somewhat, I'm afraid. But I hope to be roofing this weekend if the weather holds."

The bell began to ring. Not the mechanical kind used in most cities now, but the old-fashioned brass bell that had been around since Heather was a little girl. Her gaze shot to the clock on the wall: 9:00 a.m. sharp. Russ released her hands.

"And so it begins…"

She nodded. Another year. What would it bring? A roomful of new children, a child of her own. And what about T.J.? Would they be able to forge a happy partnership together?

Time would tell about everything, Heather knew. But as the first sneakered feet began to thunder in the wooden-floored hall, she put aside those worries.

Class was about to begin....

KAREN BOYCHUK'S BROTHERS, Paul and Perry, were going to be two of her biggest challenges this year, Heather soon realized. And two of her biggest joys. Paul was studious, like his sister, but he couldn't seem to stop himself from talking out loud whenever he became excited about something, which seemed to be often.

His brother was quieter, but the mischievous twinkle in his eyes guaranteed he would make his own impact in the classroom. He wore glasses, which was the only way, other than clothing, she saw to differentiate between the identical, curly-headed twins.

After lunch, though, she learned she wouldn't be able to rely on even that crutch.

"Perry, I'm afraid you'll have to put that yo-yo away until the bell rings."

Allie and Nicole Gibson giggled. Heather frowned, wondering what she'd missed.

"Perry?" She walked toward the boy, who was grinning widely. Then stopped when she realized he'd been sitting in the other row before the lunch bell. Her gaze swung to the left and she saw round-eyed Paul.

Or was it, Perry?

"You switched your glasses..."

Snickers turned to deep laughter. Only Perry and Paul kept an earnest expression on their faces.

Heather scooped the yo-yo from the child she now realized was, indeed, Paul. He had the red T-shirt today.

"Very funny, boys. You must drive your poor mother crazy."

"And our sister," Paul volunteered. "And our dad, and grandma and…"

"I get the picture." She smiled despite herself, then shook her head.

What would she do tomorrow when they came in with different outfits? She studied each boy, searching for something that she could count on. Finally she noticed a mole on the side of Paul's neck. That would do for now, until she became more familiar with their voices and mannerisms.

It was a fun day, without too much serious stuff on the agenda. Still, by three-thirty she could tell the kids were anxious to be free. She waved them off, but Paul and Perry hung behind.

"We're not supposed to take the bus today," Perry said. "Karen's picking us up and taking us to Yorkton for new shoes."

"Your mother working, is she?" Heather gave the boys jobs to do while they waited. Perry cleaned the boards, and Paul sorted name tags into alphabetical order. Heather was gathering her papers, when Karen stepped into the classroom.

"Hey, Ms. Sweeney." Her gaze shot over to the board, where her brother was just erasing the name

Heather had written earlier that morning. "I mean, Ms. Collins," she corrected herself quickly.

"Hi, Karen. How was the first day of grade twelve?" Heather had to force herself not to stare at her former student. Karen looked hot, hot, hot, in a pair of hip-hugging shorts and a tank top that didn't cover her navel. Heather was pretty sure neither garment met the dress code at Chatsworth High. Maybe she should be glad she just had to worry about the tricky twins in her class.

"It was fine. Actually," Karen leaned over Heather's desk and confided, "I can't wait for the year to be over."

"You're planning to go to university, of course." With Karen's marks, it would be a shame if she didn't.

"Yeah. I have an aunt who lives in Edmonton, so I might go to the University of Alberta."

"That's a fine school. What are you thinking of studying?"

They talked for a while about Karen's prospects. The twins finished their chores and grew bored. "We'll wait outside in the playground."

Heather thought Karen would leave then, but she seemed in the mood to chat. "Ryan wants to study law, isn't that amazing? He's so smart, I'll bet he gets accepted, no problem."

"If you're interested in law, why not apply yourself when the time comes? I'm sure you'll stand an excellent chance.''

''Me? Do you really think so?''

''Absolutely.'' It worried Heather that Karen didn't seem to have as much confidence in herself as she did in Ryan.

''It would be pretty cool to go to law school with Ryan.''

''Law school would be pretty cool with or without Ryan.''

Karen laughed. ''Now you sound like my parents. They think we're too serious. They just don't understand how wonderful Ryan is. And how lucky I am to be with him. Did you ever feel so crazy about a guy, he was almost always on your mind?''

Heather knew her smile was rueful. ''I think maybe I did.''

''Ryan is just so gorgeous. I love the way his eyes sparkle when he smiles. The other girls in my class would kill to go out with him. But I'm lucky—he doesn't even look at anyone else.''

Lucky, indeed. Karen, with her streaked blond hair and light blue eyes, her youthful, curvy figure and her open, trusting heart, was a prize any guy would covet.

''Your first crush is always special,'' Heather said, diplomatically.

''This isn't a crush. I'm in love. Totally in love.''

Heather smiled. Who could tell? Maybe Karen was

right and her relationship with Ryan would turn out to be a real and lasting love. It hadn't worked that way for Heather and Russ. But there were plenty of examples of high school sweethearts going on to have long, happy marriages. Adrienne and Ernie for one. Bernie English, the grade-two teacher, and her husband Chad for another.

Maybe Ryan and Karen would be among the fortunate ones.

ALL DAY AT WORK, T.J.'s guilt followed him like a dark cloud around his head. His first week as a husband had not been a success. He'd started out with a misstep when he'd turned down Heather's offer of breakfast that first morning.

Why had he been so damn rude? It would have been easy enough to sit down and drink some coffee and eat an egg or two. That's all it would have taken to please her.

But he didn't want to set her up to expect more than he was capable of delivering in the long haul. When he'd been married to Lynn, he'd always been out the door before she and the baby woke up. At night, Sally was often asleep by the time he returned.

His hours at the hardware weren't nearly as onerous. Still, it would be misleading to give Heather the impression that she'd married a nine-to-five man.

Hell, he'd warned her from the beginning, hadn't he?

But since today was her first day back at school, he had planned to get home in time to help make dinner. Then a truckload of merchandise arrived from Winnipeg in the late afternoon, and he knew he wouldn't be able to get away. In fact, it was almost eight by the time he'd locked up the store and began to take the unaccustomed route to her house on Mallard Avenue.

It had made sense for him to move from his small apartment to her house, rather than the other way around, but he still felt strange about the situation. Not that he didn't like Heather's place. She kept things casual and fun with lots of color and comfortable furniture. But every time he walked in the front door, he felt almost overwhelmed. Her personality, her scent, her beauty were stamped into each room of the place.

Even before he opened the front door, he could hear music, Dixie Chicks he thought. That was something he'd learned about her this past week. She didn't watch much TV. She preferred music, usually country, sometimes rock.

He locked the door behind himself, hung up his keys, removed his shoes. The living room was empty, so he walked through to the kitchen. Heather sat at the table, bouncing to the title track, head bent over some papers.

"Have you eaten?"

She started. "Oh. I didn't hear you come in."

"The music's a little loud."

"I'll turn it down." She leaned over to adjust the controls on the stereo in the cabinet right by the table. "Have you eaten?"

"That's what I just asked you." He noticed the nonstick frying pan on the stove and a plate with bread crumbs next to the dishwasher. Heather was not a clean-as-you-go kind of cook.

"I had a grilled cheese sandwich a while ago." She glanced at the clock.

"Sounds good to me." As he made his own meal, he thought how strange it was to be living with someone again. Strange, but nice, too. He glanced at Heather—his *wife*—and saw that she was watching him. She smiled, then lowered her gaze to the page again.

What did she think about the situation? He didn't have the nerve to ask. At least she didn't seem to be holding a grudge about the other morning. Maybe she could see that the best way for them to make this work was to each go about their own business, as much like before as possible.

He carried his plate to the table. At first she continued to work. Finally he asked, "How was the first day?"

She pushed aside her papers and told him about a set of twins who sounded like they were going to be a real handful, then about their knockout sister, Karen—he'd seen her in the hardware store a few times, and she looked too sexy for her own good—and then about the principal's plans for the year. A part of him listened, a part just enjoyed watching her talk. The way she moved her hands, tilted her head, the expressions on her open face. Mannerisms he knew intimately, yet felt he could never see enough of.

At work he needed only to think of her and he immediately grew hot. The sexy, adorable girl he'd always wanted—almost all his life—was going to be in his bed every night. He didn't think he would ever tire in his delight of her body.

It was the in-between times that made him worry. As soon as he finished his meal, Heather bent over her papers again. He whisked away his plate then cleaned the kitchen.

By the time he was done, Heather had finished her work. She piled the papers into the briefcase she carried to and from school, then smiled uncertainly.

He knew how she felt. What now? "Want to watch TV?"

"Not really. I'm kind of tired." She yawned, as if to prove the point, then pushed herself out of her chair.

As she straightened, the fabric of her dress pulled across her belly. Her pregnancy was just starting to show there, but what drew his eyes were her breasts. They'd always been generous, but now they seemed to him fully ripe and glorious.

"Bed, then?" He shifted his gaze away from hers, slightly uncomfortable, but also excited. Was every night too often for her? She hadn't complained yet, had certainly seemed to be enjoying herself. But he remembered how Lynn had pushed him away those first months of pregnancy. She'd been so fatigued and sick. And he hadn't really minded. Her going to bed early had made it possible for him to stay up late working.

But even though he had orders to process and bills to organize for his accountant, he didn't want to work tonight.

## CHAPTER EIGHT

HEATHER TOOK HER TURN in the bathroom, brushing her teeth, washing her face. Knowing T.J. was waiting outside the door made her hurry through the routine.

Bed was the one place where she truly felt like T.J.'s wife. The one place where he seemed to open up a little, exposing the softer side that so far she'd only glimpsed.

Otherwise, they were more like roommates than husband and wife. He didn't kiss her when he came home from work. And apparently it didn't occur to him to phone her when he was going to be at the store late. Which seemed to be more nights than not.

He'd warned her about all this, of course. But she couldn't believe how annoying she found it, nonetheless. What good was having a husband if you didn't have him around to keep you company during dinner, or to go on a stroll through town in the early evening? Was their whole married life going to be like this? Separate meals, separate lives, separate everything…until bedtime.

She stepped out of the bathroom in a white cotton

nightgown she'd owned forever. She didn't think it was especially glamorous, but T.J.—already sitting in bed—seemed to find the sight of her in it riveting.

He was the gorgeous one. Broad shoulders, strong chest, tapering to a narrow waist. And those piercing blue eyes.

"You're beautiful," he said.

He was generous with his compliments, but only in bed, she'd noticed. Why was it only in the intimacy of this room that he could show her the affection a man should have for his wife?

He held the covers open for her and she crawled in beside him. She wondered if they would ever cuddle together to watch a movie, hold hands in the café, rub suntan lotion onto each other's bodies at the beach, the way Karen and Ryan had done.

She sighed.

"What's wrong?"

T.J. had been massaging her shoulders, now he pulled back to examine her face. "Are you too tired?"

She considered saying yes but didn't have the willpower to deny herself the only affection and intimacy that her husband appeared willing to give her.

"No, I'm not too tired." She turned to him, and minutes later shuddered with the exquisite perfection of his kiss.

T.J. LOVED HOLDING HEATHER close after they made love, but he made sure not to do it for too long.

Lynn had always slept better when they were on separate sides of the bed. Especially when she was pregnant.

Just as he was reluctantly opening his arms to let her go, Heather turned to him, her eyelids dragging with fatigue.

"Did I tell you I have a four o'clock doctor's appointment tomorrow?"

"Not that I recall." He watched her shift about a foot away from him. She tucked her hand under her pillow and settled a cheek into downy softness.

"It's my monthly checkup. I wondered if—" she plucked a tiny feather from the sheet between them "—if you might like to come," she added in a rush.

He closed his eyes. At first, Lynn had invited him along to her checkups. But something always got in the way. An appointment he couldn't miss, an important business lunch, a court date.

"I can't."

"Can't? Or won't?"

Her eyes were wide open now, reflecting disapproval, and worse, disappointment.

"I told you I was no good with things like this. Look, it's better I just be up front and say I'm not coming. Otherwise, I'd get busy at the last second, or just plain forget, and then you'd be disappointed."

"Is that really your reason?" She sounded annoyed.

"Yes."

"Your logic is pretty shaky, T.J. And so are your priorities."

"Yeah, well, I love you, too, sweetheart."

She expelled a breath in a loud huff of censure, then flipped to her other side. It was a marital move that he remembered all too clearly. It meant, *I'm giving up on you and going to sleep now.*

So he closed his eyes and tried to do the same. But it was hard. Because a part of him really wanted to do the checkup thing with Heather tomorrow. But he knew that even if he did manage to leave work on time and get her to the appointment, he'd find some other way of screwing up. At least, that was his usual pattern. With marriage. And with Heather.

TWO WEEKS PASSED AND SOON Heather had an established schedule in the classroom, and a much less satisfactory one at home. More often than not, T.J. worked past dinnertime. As he'd promised, he put in hours at the hardware most Saturdays and often a part of Sunday.

When he was free, he took long runs around the lake or worked out on his weights which he'd set up in the basement. He had a TV connected to cable down there, too. He said it was so she could listen to her music without interruption. But she guessed he preferred to be alone.

One evening as she prowled the living room in

boredom, it occurred to her that she hadn't had to make so much as one change to accommodate T.J.'s belongings into her home. His weights and TV, and a few boxes of storage, had gone to the basement, which she only used for laundry. He'd put his clothes in the spare bedroom closet and bureau, and added his books to her mostly empty shelving unit in that room. But other than that, he'd brought nothing with him.

Not a favorite chair from which he couldn't bear to part. No ugly sporting trophies. Not even a coffee mug.

The apartment over the hardware store had been furnished, but still. You'd think he'd have a few special belongings. At least a picture of his daughter.

Heather wandered to the bedroom. T.J. was working out downstairs. The clothes he'd worn to the store were already in the laundry hamper. He was actually a much neater person than she was. She picked up the long, flowing dress she'd worn earlier and slipped it onto a padded hanger.

Her gaze swept past the closet to the table at T.J.'s side of the bed. He'd taken off his watch and removed his wallet from the back pocket of his jeans where he usually kept it. She picked up the wallet. The leather, a buttery-brown color, was soft from years of use. She flipped it open.

He had one neat row of cards, including a VISA and driver's license. She stared at his photo, mesmerized by the power of his eyes. In a separate compartment she found some money—a few bills, not many. Which left a zippered pouch. She opened it and pulled out the one photo contained within.

The baby girl was a toddler, dressed in a pink cotton dress, a fancy hair band around her head making up for the fact that she had only tufts of dark hair. She had deep blue eyes like her daddy.

Heather flipped over the photo. There was nothing inscribed but she knew, of course, that this was Sally.

"If you need money, Heather, I'd prefer you just ask."

An involuntary sound of surprise escaped from her mouth. She swiveled and found T.J. standing in the doorway.

"I—"

She couldn't think of anything to say. Really, there was no excuse for what she'd done. He knew she wasn't after his money. So far they didn't even have a joint bank account. As with most other aspects of their lives, financially they continued to live as if they weren't even married. Mutely she handed him his wallet. And the photo.

He frowned as he tucked the picture back into the zipper compartment.

"If you had a bigger picture we could frame it for the wall," she offered. She had a bunch of family photos, including her university degree, grouped on a wall in her living room.

"Heather, don't. Okay?" T.J. tossed his wallet back onto the night table. "I'm going to take a shower."

She couldn't believe he wasn't going to discuss this further. She watched in amazement as he headed for the bathroom, then closed the door.

She sank onto the bed and waited for her breathing to return to normal. What was wrong with that man? Didn't he love his daughter? But he must. He *had* to.

Fifteen minutes later when T.J. emerged, his body damp, a towel slung around his waist, she was still sitting there.

"When's your next visit to Toronto?"

T.J. stopped in his tracks. "I don't have anything planned."

"When's the last time you saw Sally?"

"A year ago. No," he revised, "more like eighteen months."

Heather couldn't imagine how long eighteen months must feel to a four-year-old. "She probably doesn't even remember you."

"I know."

"Doesn't that bother you?"

He dropped his towel, showing absolutely no self-consciousness about being naked. "What I feel doesn't matter. She has a father in her life. I showed you the pictures. She'd only be confused if I kept dropping into her life, then disappearing again. It's better this way."

Was he for real? "Better that she never sees her real father?"

"Maybe when she's older she'll be able to deal with it."

"When she's older it will be too late!"

T.J. turned back the covers. "I guess you're entitled to your opinion. But she's my daughter. And I think this way is best. She's happy. She has a mother and a father. There's no room in her life for me."

Did he honestly believe that was true? Heather watched as he turned out the lamp on his side, then slid into bed. As soon as his head settled on the pillow, he closed his eyes.

Only the pulsing vein in his neck gave any sign that his emotions were engaged.

Silently Heather sat and waited for him to say something else. He didn't. She thought about what that could mean. Maybe he didn't care, but she doubted that was true. More likely he had to keep his feelings so tightly contained in order to prevent himself from being overwhelmed.

But he couldn't carry on this way. Not only was it not fair to Sally, but it wasn't healthy for him, either.

Or their marriage. Until he resolved his feelings about his relationships with Sally and her mother, and devised a reasonable plan to be a part of his daughter's life, Heather was afraid he would never be able to commit totally to her or their baby.

With a heavy sigh, Heather headed for the bathroom. When she returned from her nightly preparations, she found her husband's back turned toward her. From the sound of his even breathing, it seemed he was asleep.

And so, for the first time in their married life, they went to sleep without making love.

A FEW DAYS LATER, after the last bell, Karen Boychuk came to Heather's class again to pick up her brothers.

"I think they must be out in the playground." Heather was gathering her students' story journals to read over the weekend. Not tonight, though. She and Adrienne had a date to see a movie in Yorkton.

With three young kids, her friend rarely had a free evening, but apparently every one of her children was staying at someone else's house for a sleepover and Ernie had the late night shift at the mine.

"Yeah, I saw them on the monkey bars, but thought I'd come up and see how you're doing. I heard you were pregnant," she added, shyly.

Heather smiled. "Yes, I am. And I'm doing just fine, thank you."

It was close to the end of September now, and the weather was turning cooler. Karen wore jeans today, the kind that were cut below her hipbones. Not that long ago, Heather's waist would have rivaled the young girl's in slenderness. But no longer. Just last Saturday Heather had been forced to buy a whole batch of maternity wear. She had on a pair of pants now with a stretch panel over her tummy. A pale pink knit top with long sleeves and a scooped neck fell to the top of her thighs, covering the panel.

"Can you feel the baby moving yet?" Karen sat on the top of one of the desks, letting her foot dangle in the air.

"Sometimes I think I can feel a little fluttering."

"How cool. Have you seen an ultrasound?"

"My doctor is recommending we wait another month for that."

"Will you want to know the sex?"

"I'm not sure. I hadn't thought about it much." She could ask T.J. for his opinion, but her guess was he wouldn't care. And that hurt. Why, Karen was showing more interest in this baby than he had so far. She'd thought she could handle his halfhearted commitment to their marriage, but it was proving much more difficult than she'd imagined.

"I'd like to have kids someday," Karen said. "Four. Two girls and two boys."

Heather smiled. Funny how when you were young you thought you could just order them up that way. Two girls and two boys. But Adrienne, who'd been dying to have a girl she could pamper and primp, had ended up with three sons. And Chad and Bernie

English had just had their second daughter. After a while, it didn't seem to matter what sex the kids were. They were loved no matter what.

"You have plenty of time, Karen."

"Yeah, I suppose." Karen jumped off the desk and prowled the classroom. She appeared to be examining the art work hanging on the walls, but Heather guessed something else was on her mind.

"How do you know when you've met the guy who's going to be *the one*? Is it something you figure out right away? Or does the feeling sort of grow over time?"

Oh, no. *Why me?* Heather prayed for the wisdom to handle this correctly. "I'm sure it happens both ways. But I'd be more inclined to trust the feelings that grow over time."

"That's me and Ryan." Karen sighed, dreamily. "The more I get to know him, the crazier I feel about him. Tell me the truth, Ms. Collins. Have you ever seen a better looking guy?"

Well, not Russell. He was attractive, but not handsome in a traditional sense. Even her love, strong as it had been, hadn't blinded her to that.

T.J., though. T.J. came close. But Heather knew Karen wasn't really searching for an answer to her question. "There are more important qualities to look for in a boyfriend, Karen."

Again, her husband was the perfect example. What good did his movie-star appeal do her when she had to eat yet another meal on her own? Or go out to the movies with a girlfriend because he always worked late?

"I know, but Ryan has everything. He's smart and outgoing and good at sports."

"Well, I hope—" Heather didn't get a chance to finish her sentence. Because the subject of their conversation had appeared in her room. Ryan Farrell grinned at her from the doorway, putting her in mind of Johnny Depp in his earlier TV days.

Heather could see what Karen found so attractive, all right. She smiled at her former student. "Never thought I'd see you in my classroom again, Ryan."

"Now that you're married, I wouldn't have thought so, either, Ms. Collins." He worked his way next to his girlfriend, slipped an arm around her neck. Karen obviously didn't mind the possessive gesture.

"Hey, Ryan. I thought you were going home?"

"Changed my mind. Thought I might give you a hand with those terror brothers of yours." He looked back at Heather, including her in the conversation. "I still can't tell those kids apart."

"Paul's the talkative one," Karen explained. "Perry's the one who plans all the mischief. You can tell when you look at his eyes really closely."

"I know exactly what you mean," Heather said, laughing a little. "Today Paul must have spent fifteen minutes giving me the answer to a simple science question. Meanwhile, Perry mixed the contents of two test tubes and created the worst smell ever. He was quite pleased with himself, though not so happy when I made him wash out the test tubes.''

''Sounds like Perry,'' Karen agreed.

''Ready to go?'' Ryan pulled her toward the door.

''Sure. Have a good weekend, Ms. Collins.''

Heather went to the doorway, her gaze lingering as they strolled down the hall like Siamese twins. They did make an adorable couple. She had an urge to wrap them in cotton batting, to protect the fragile innocence of their love from the hard knocks that real life would be sure to deliver.

## CHAPTER NINE

SATURDAY MORNING HEATHER made pancakes and sausages for breakfast. She told herself she didn't care if T.J. ate them or not. It was the weekend and she was hungry. Ten minutes later, T.J. strode in from his run. He stood in the kitchen in his running clothes, his hair damp with sweat. "I have to be at work in half an hour."

She shrugged. "No one's forcing you to eat."

That definitely took him aback.

"Is there enough for two?"

She nodded.

"Let me take a quick shower first. Won't be more than five minutes."

True to his word, he was back at the table shortly, this time dressed in his usual black jeans and T-shirt. Heather served first his plate, then her own. T.J. helped himself to coffee. She'd stopped drinking anything with caffeine and had made herself herbal tea.

After T.J. finished his last bite, she brought out a plastic bag from under her chair and set it on the table in front of him.

"When I was in town last night, I bought you a little present."

"Yeah?" He looked at the bag suspiciously.

"Go ahead. Open it."

He stuffed the last bit of pancake into his mouth, then pushed aside his plate and reached for the bag. He pulled out the album first, then two disposable cameras.

"What's this for?"

"I had an idea." Heather took their dirty plates and carried them to the dishwasher. "Sally's too young to read or write yet. But maybe you could communicate through pictures. I thought you could mail one of those cameras to her. Ask her to take pictures of her life in Toronto and send them to you. Meanwhile, you can take your own photos and make a little album to give her."

T.J. stared at her.

"It can be a way for the two of you to get to know each other, even though you're so far apart."

"Heather... I told you to stay out of this."

She hadn't expected him to embrace the idea. But she hadn't anticipated anger, either.

"I heard the idea on a TV show—"

"I don't care where you got the idea. This isn't about you. Why can't you understand that?" He pushed away from the table and stormed toward the door.

Heather followed. "What is the matter with you?

Why are you always pushing people away? I was only trying to help. And I think—"

"Don't. Okay? Don't think at all. Just concentrate on being a cute little redhead. 'Cause that's something you're really good at."

He opened the door and stepped outside. She was right behind him, slamming the door before he had a chance to close it. Damn him and his arrogant attitude. No wonder his first marriage had failed. No wonder Lynn had given up on him. Heather didn't remember seeing this chauvinistic side of him before, but it disgusted her.

And confused her, too.

Last night, when she'd come home late from the movie, she'd found him in bed, waiting for her. They'd made love and he'd been especially tender and loving. It was so hard for her to reconcile these two sides of T.J. In bed he showed her so much respect. He was always giving, giving, giving.

Then, he turned around and talked to her like this. She didn't get it. She didn't get it at all.

BY THE TIME T.J. REACHED the store, he was ready to admit, to himself at least, that he'd been an asshole. Heather had tried to do something sweet for him, with the best of motives, and he'd retaliated with a launch of verbal abuse that she certainly didn't deserve.

What a jerk.

Almost on autopilot, he unlocked the front door, powered on the lights, then flipped over the Closed sign. Don Arbuckle, a man about five years older than T.J. who'd worked for his father since he graduated high school, wasn't here yet, so T.J. swept the front sidewalk, then went inside to turn on the till.

At the counter, he saw the latest postcard from his parents, a scenic view of the bridge that connected Prince Edward Island to Nova Scotia. "We were here!" his mother had scrawled on the back of the card. He could imagine the glee she'd felt writing those words.

He'd never had a postcard, or letter, or note of any kind from Heather. But he guessed that she would have that same exuberant style. Lots of exclamation marks and smiley faces and x's and o's. Her happy nature was one of the qualities that had always fascinated him.

He stopped in his tracks, put a hand to his head. He really had been an asshole this morning. She was sweet and kind, and her intentions had been good—why did he have to blast her that way?

He'd get her a present, he decided. To show he was sorry. He picked out a pretty vase from the housewares section. He could fill this with some of the flowers blooming in his mom's garden. No one was there to enjoy them, anyway.

Would flowers in a vase do the trick? He hoped so. He didn't want to hurt Heather. But somehow he had to make her understand that the damage to his relationship with his daughter was irreparable.

Oh, maybe under different circumstances he could make amends for pretty much ignoring her the first four years of her existence. But Toronto was so far away, a two-day drive, at the very least. And even to fly wasn't easy, as Chatsworth was several hours from the closest airport.

Still, he would have made the effort. Of course he would have. But Lynn's husband, Jeff, was such a perfect father already. Sally had everything she needed from him: attention, approval, love. All the things T.J. had never provided.

The front door opened, and he looked up to see Henry Bateson wander in. The old farmer had on a freshly pressed work shirt and even his well-worn pants had a neat crease down each leg.

"Looking sharp, Henry. Your new wife must be taking good care of you." Henry, a widower, had recently remarried. He lived in town now but still went out to the farm to help his daughter Libby and her husband Gibson on a regular basis.

"Oh, Sue's a pretty terrific cook and good with the laundry, too," Henry agreed. "She's also a hell of a golfer. We're hoping to get out for a round later this afternoon, but first I need to go out to Libby and Gibson's. Do you have 2 x 3/8 inch bolts with lock washers and nuts? I stripped the old ones when I was tightening the pickup belts on Gibson's combine yesterday.''

''I'm sure I do. Let's go to the bins at the back and check. What's Gibson got planted on that quarter this year? Canola?''

''Yeah. The yield looks pretty good, too. He'll have it all in today, if everything goes well.''

The chimes on the front door sounded, signaling Don Arbuckle's arrival. He nodded at T.J. and Henry then went straight to work processing orders. After Henry left with the parts he'd needed, Abe Farrell showed up needing supplies to repair some granaries on a section of land a few kilometers from his home. His youngest son, Ryan, carried everything out to the truck, while Abe paid with his credit card.

''Nice to have your son around to help,'' T.J. commented, nodding in the direction that Ryan had just left.

''Not for long. That one's headed for university soon's he gets his high school diploma,'' Abe said. ''He's good with books, always has been. His older brother is the farmer. He'll take over from me one day.''

''You have a third son, too, don't you?''

Abe nodded. ''He's working at the mine. Seems to be happy doing that.''

A steady stream of customers kept T.J. occupied for most of the morning. Then at noon, T.J. took over the till, while Don went to the café for lunch. At one,

Don returned and patted T.J. on the back. "Your turn, buddy."

"Thanks." T.J. used the break to pick flowers at his mother's. Then he took the vase home and placed it on the table.

While he was there, he made himself a sandwich, poured a tall glass of milk and took his meal to the back patio. Early frost had claimed some of the more delicate blooms in the terra-cotta pots that Heather had placed haphazardly around the old teak lawn furniture. Beyond the patio, a dense growth of trees and shrubs allowed only patches of grass to survive. She had a couple of bird feeders nailed to the trees, and a birdhouse, too. The birdhouse was empty now, the babies having all learned to fly long ago.

T.J.'s mother kept her yard perfectly manicured and groomed. But this way had its advantages. Sitting out here, you could barely tell you were in town. He leaned his head back and breathed deeply. Though most nights were dipping below zero degrees, right now the sun felt hot on his face, and the house shielded him from the cool breeze.

It was so peaceful, he almost fell asleep. Then a neighbor's dog started to bark, and a woman—Mrs. Manley from across the street?—yelled at the poor creature to be quiet. T.J. leaned forward in his chair, finished his sandwich with one big bite, then returned to the house.

He rinsed his dishes and wiped down the counter.

On his way out the door he paused and looked back at the table. There, next to the vase of fresh-picked flowers, were the cameras Heather had bought him.

He put them back into the shopping bag, then thrust the bag into the closet in the spare room. Again, he went to leave, and again he paused at the front door.

Oh, what the hell.

He marched to the bedroom and yanked down the bag. He removed one of the disposable cameras and dropped it into the pocket of his light jacket.

He didn't think about what he was going to do with the camera. He didn't make any plans at all. Just closed the closet door and made his way quickly back to the store.

ON HIS WAY HOME THAT NIGHT, about seven-thirty in the evening, T.J. took a detour along Lakeshore Drive starting at the memorial statue where Main Street met the water's edge. He paused in front of the construction at the Matthews' house. The exterior was pretty much completed now. During the day the workers would be drywalling inside, but right now the place was quiet. Everyone had gone home for the evening.

It was a nice looking place. Wide windows made the house seem friendly. The generous front veran-dah was cozy and welcoming.

T.J. had noticed Heather's interest in this house.

She stopped frequently to check on its progress. That wasn't so unusual. Many people in Chatsworth were curious. They didn't see a lot of new construction in town.

But Heather's fascination, he was sure, went beyond the idle nosiness of most of their neighbors. He had a theory. He guessed she couldn't stop wishing that it was for *her* Russell was building this house.

It was obviously meant to be a family home. A place where children would play happily and return to with warm memories once they'd left to go to university or taken a job in a faraway city.

He could picture Heather living in a house like this. It was the lifestyle she'd always craved. And Russell was the man she'd always wanted.

T.J. had lived with that knowledge forever. Even after all she'd gone through—having Russ's baby on her own, giving it up for adoption, standing by while Russ married someone else—there was a hint of reverence in Heather's voice when she spoke Russell's name. A secret part of her seemed to come alive when she was in his presence.

He'd noticed the signs at the annual Harvest Festival last year. And the year before. He guessed Julie saw the same thing he did. She and Heather kept a wide berth between them.

T.J. was just turning to leave, when, unexpectedly, the front door opened. Julie Matthew stepped out onto the porch. She wore what T.J. considered city clothes. Tailored slacks, a white blouse that looked freshly ironed even though it was the end of the day. As she drew closer he saw she wore a beautiful silver necklace with a bold turquoise pendant. It was the sort of jewelry that would look awful on nine out of ten women who wore it. Of course, Julie Matthew was the one in ten who could carry it off.

"T.J. I didn't see you at first. It's getting dark earlier and earlier these days, isn't it?"

They'd gotten to know each other shortly after Julie and Russ had moved to town. Julie had come to his store to buy paint. He liked Julie, though he knew not everyone in town did. Some thought she was stuck-up. He knew she wasn't. But having lived most of her life as the privileged daughter of a wealthy businessman in London, England, she couldn't help being different.

"Your house is coming along. It's going to look great."

She glanced over her shoulder, assessed what she saw for a moment, then turned back to him. "Yes, I'm very pleased. I was just inside, checking the window measurements for the blinds. I'm ordering them from Vancouver and don't want to make any errors."

She wouldn't, T.J. thought. Julie wasn't the kind to rush a job or make impulsive decisions.

Heather would, though. And if she happened to measure wrong, or whatever, she'd just laugh and make the best of it.

"When are you planning on moving in?" He saw Julie's Volvo at the side of the road and went to open the door for her.

"We hope in time for Christmas. Maybe sooner. We're living with Russell's parents and I'm sure you can imagine what that's like."

There were few secrets in a small town. Most everyone knew that Betty Matthew wouldn't have chosen a city-girl like Julie to be her son's wife. She would have been far more approving of his first girlfriend—Heather.

"I heard she softened some after Emma was born."

Julie smiled. "She's a wonderful grandma, I'll say that for her. I think it would be hard on anyone, being forced to live with parents again. Russell and I have our own ways of doing things..." She sighed. "Oh, well. It's only for another couple of months. How are things with you? Married life suiting you okay?"

"It's fine."

She waited a moment, as if expecting him to say something else, then slid into the driver's seat in one elegant motion. She glanced up at him. "Nice to see you, T.J. Take care."

"Yeah. You, too." He closed the door for her, then watched her drive off. Finally he was faced with the prospect of going home. He couldn't put it off any longer.

He hoped the flowers had done the trick.

## CHAPTER TEN

"He tried to buy me off with flowers, Adrienne. At least his first wife got a diamond bracelet."

Heather crossed her arms in front of her chest. She and her friend were in the café, at a window booth, and Donna had just served them tall chocolate shakes with whipping cream and cherries on top.

"You don't like diamonds," Adrienne pointed out.

"Well, I might like them if there were a lot of them. In a row. Surrounded by gold."

"Where would you wear a bracelet like that?"

"To church. To parties. To the Harvest Festival." It was coming up in a few short weeks. Somehow Heather had ended up with the unenviable job of decorating the town hall for the event.

"You couldn't wear it with that watch."

Heather glanced at her freckled wrist. No, she could see that a diamond tennis bracelet and a plastic pink-and-blue watch wouldn't really go together.

"Forget the bracelet. That isn't the point."

"If you don't mind me asking... What *is* the point? I'd be pretty happy if Ernie bought me flow-

ers—even if they were just picked out of his
mother's garden. It's, well, it's romantic.''

"The *point,* Adrienne, the *point* is that he didn't
say he was sorry. He as good as called me a bubble-
headed sex toy and never even apologized.''

"Maybe he thought you would be complimented
that he considers you sexy. I can sure see why.''
Adrienne's gaze dropped to Heather's chest. "Tell
me, do they even *make* bras that big?''

Heather glared at her. She knew her face was
blooming with color. "Adrienne…''

"Sorry, I can't help being curious, never having
had to look past the A cups in my life. Oh, except
when I was pregnant and breastfeeding, of course. I
exploded all the way to B cups then. Ernie was one
happy man.''

Heather had to laugh. "Adrienne, you're impossible.''

"I try.'' She took a long drink of her shake. "So
what did T.J. say when he came home from work?
Did he make any reference, at all, to what happened?''

"Nope. He waltzed in the door—it was already
after eight—and didn't say a thing. Not a word. Just
did his usual dinner in front of the TV routine.''

She stirred her milkshake with a long spoon and
tried not to glance outside in the direction of the
Handy Hardware.

Another Saturday on her own. Why had she even

bothered to get married? They were never together. But that was probably a good thing. When they did spend a few moments in the same room—provided it wasn't the bedroom—they soon ran out of things to talk about.

"You know what, Adrienne? I don't even like him anymore."

"What are you talking about? You never did like him."

"Oh, yeah. So why did I marry him again?"

Adrienne leaned over the table and spoke in a whisper. "You married him because you made a baby together. And because you find him incredibly attractive."

"And because *you* told me to!" Suddenly she recalled something T.J. had told her. "I didn't know you had coffee with T.J. every morning."

Adrienne waved a hand dismissively. "It's a casual thing. We just show up at the same time, along with a bunch of other people."

"Including Julie?"

"Well, yeah. Sometimes."

Heather told herself it was crazy to be jealous. "What do you talk about?"

"Just stuff. Nothing serious."

"Does he ever mention me?"

"Oh, Heather."

He didn't.

"You've got to give him a chance. It's only been a month—"

"Seven weeks."

"Whatever. Give this some time, Heather. You need to get to know each other."

"We've known each other since we were four years old." They'd gone to the same play group together. "How much longer do you think it'll take?" She spooned the cherry off the top of her drink, then popped it into her mouth.

"Another month? A year? Who cares? I just know that you have to make this work."

"Easy for you to say. You're married to Ernie. That man agrees with everything you say. He thinks you walk on water." Ernie was probably the only person she'd ever heard compliment Adrienne on her hair color. When he looked at his wife, he saw only the very best.

Whereas she and T.J. seemed to see only the very worst in each other.

"I'd suggest we try counseling, but I know what he'd say. He almost exploded when I brought up the idea of him talking to someone about his ex-wife and child."

"That's a good idea. He probably has a lot of unresolved issues there."

"I know he does. But he won't go." She balled up a tissue, then tossed it into the ashtray at the next table.

Lucky, the owner of the grocery store across the street, who'd been craning his neck to hear, just shook his head at her and continued to enjoy his coffee and pie.

"Maybe we should have the two of you over for dinner," Adrienne said. "It might help if you start going out as a couple."

"Maybe." It was true T.J. behaved slightly better when they went for Sunday dinners to her parents. But it wasn't because he enjoyed spending the time with her. He and her dad had really hit it off. They enjoyed conversing about things like organic gardening and the implications of genetically altered foods. Topics Heather could enjoy for half an hour, but not much longer than that.

A couple of boys dashed into the café, laughing with excitement.

"What are you going to get?" one asked the other.

"I dunno. Maybe bubblegum. Or cookies and cream."

The Boychuk twins, Paul and Perry. Heather discarded her initial impulse to duck under the table. "Hi, boys. Out for a little ice cream, I see."

In tandem, they swung their faces in her direction. She felt a tingle of gratitude to see them both break out in wide smiles.

"Ms. Collins! We didn't see you sitting there. What did you order? Is it chocolate? Why aren't you drinking it—it's gonna melt and go all watery. Would you like another straw?''

That was Paul, of course. Perry was carefully casing the place. Looking for trouble, no doubt.

''Where's your sister today?''

''With Ryan,'' Paul said. ''She's always with Ryan.'' He and his brother made kissy noises, then rolled their eyes and laughed.

''They're sitting by the war statue at the end of Main Street,'' Perry elaborated. ''Ryan gave us some money to get ice cream. Told us not to come back for a good hour. Like either of us has a watch.''

Just beyond the statue, which had been built to commemorate the local men who had died in the two World Wars, was a bank of grass leading down to the lake. It was a quiet spot, Heather remembered, surrounded by willows and a stand of poplars. The perfect place for a young couple to make out for a while.

''Here.'' She dug in her pocket for another couple of dollars. ''Why don't you surprise them and get them some ice cream, too?''

Paul looked uncertain, but Perry's eyes took on a familiar sparkle. ''Good idea, Ms. Collins. That's a really, really good idea.''

Once the boys were gone, each carrying two ice-cream cones, Adrienne shook her finger at Heather.

''That was nasty.''

''I know. But I wish Karen would spend more time

focusing on her studies rather than her boyfriend. She's a bright girl.''

"She's also eighteen. Give her a break."

The view out the window distracted Heather from their conversation. She watched a familiar man step out the front door of the Handy Hardware. "Look," she whispered, pointing for Adrienne's benefit.

Adrienne swiveled and craned her neck. She turned back, unimpressed. "So T.J. is leaving his store for a minute. Maybe he's coming here for a coffee."

"I don't think so. He's got something in his hands…" Heather watched as her husband crossed the street, then turned back to face his store. He lifted the thing he was carrying to his face, stood still for a few seconds, then ran back inside the building.

"What was that all about?" Adrienne asked.

"I think he just took a picture of his store," Heather said softly. She picked up her milkshake and put the straw to her lips. And smiled. Vindication, she decided, was much more satisfying than an apology.

THE NEXT EVENING HEATHER was dropping tablespoons of batter onto a cookie sheet, when she sensed T.J.'s presence. Lifting her head, she saw him at the other end of the table. He stood with his legs slightly apart, his hands behind his back.

"Can I ask you something?"

"They aren't even in the oven yet. But it'll only take about ten minutes."

"Not that. I wondered if you would mind if I...took your picture." He pulled out the little disposable camera she'd seen him use yesterday on the street.

"Oh." Her first instinct was to be glad. T.J. wanted his daughter to know about her. That was a very good thing.

Her second reaction was pure vanity. She didn't want his first wife to see her like this. "But I'm in my sweats. I'm not wearing any makeup. And my hair..." Even her ponytail wasn't neat. Several strands had broken free. She could feel them curling against her cheeks and her neck.

"You're perfect," T.J. said. He looked like he meant it, too.

"Well." She smiled then, and he snapped one picture, then another. He took a photo of the tray filled with mounds of cookie batter, then one of her putting the whole thing in the oven.

Later, when they were ready, he asked her to take a picture of him, biting into one fresh, delicious cookie. She pressed the button just as he took his second bite.

"That's good," he said. He had a bit of melted chocolate on his lower lip.

Heather wiped it off with the tip of her finger. Then she licked it. "Can't waste good chocolate."

T.J. finished the rest of the cookie in one huge bite. He chewed. Swallowed. Then moved close. "See any more?"

His lips were clean. But Heather figured it couldn't hurt to pretend. She put a hand on each of his shoulders, then leaned in, touching her tongue to his bottom lip. He tasted sweet. She ran her tongue along the full curve of that lip, then moved to the other one.

T.J.'s mouth parted. Soon he was checking out her lips, too, then her mouth. They kissed deeply, but thoroughly. T.J. splayed his hands against her back, running them up to her shoulders, then to her bottom, and pulling her close.

Each time he touched her she was amazed at how gentle he was. Demanding, too, but never excessively so. She wrapped her arms around him, feeling the soft cotton of his shirt, the warmth of his body. She broke away from his kisses to nuzzle her face into his neck. His skin was fragrant from the shower he'd taken after his run. She loved the way he smelled.

"Heather."

He made her name sound like a long, hot moan. Made her body feel like warm, pliable clay, ready to be molded, however he chose.

How did he do this to her? She was supposed to be mad at him. He still hadn't apologized.

He linked a hand around each of her thighs and lifted her legs up. Instinctively she wrapped them around his hips. He shifted her weight upward, until they were face-to-face.

"Don't hurt your back."

He laughed into her ear. "You're like china, Heather. Light and delicate. I could carry you for an hour, if I had to."

"Fortunately, the bed is just down the hall."

"Yes, that is lucky, isn't it?" He carried her the length of the short hall, settled her on top of the quilt.

Watching as her husband undressed first her, then himself, Heather knew they were just buying time. Their marriage couldn't last, sustained only by marvelous lovemaking. Eventually they had to talk. About real issues.

But feeling T.J.'s fingers dance over her skin, it was easy to brush away those negative thoughts. She cupped his face between her hands and gazed into his eyes. She couldn't see anything that wasn't warm, approving...loving. He'd never said the words, neither had she.

But tonight, right now, she felt love as powerfully as if it was a physical presence in the room with them.

MORNING CAME LIKE A LONG, cold shower, cleansing away the fairy dust and magic of the previous night. T.J. left for work early, calling out a curt goodbye before exiting through the front door.

It was almost as if their nights together scared him.

Or maybe, when he wasn't in the mood he just couldn't be bothered to be nice to her.

Heather went through the motions of getting ready for work. This week her belly had ''popped'' and she finally had the comforting little mound she'd longed for when she'd first realized she was pregnant. She wasn't as tired as she'd been, either, yet she didn't have her usual vim.

She suspected the underlying problems with T.J. were zapping her energy. She worried about the effect of negative thoughts. Could they possibly harm her baby?

She wanted a happy, secure child. Let life deliver him hard knocks if it must, but from his parents and his home he would have only the best.

Determinedly she turned on some lively country music by Farmer's Daughter. She danced lightly around the coffee table in the living room until she felt something bubbling inside her.

Joy.

Yes, she and T.J. had problems, but they would work them out. They were going to have a baby. She was going to be a mother. When this child was born, she would hold him in her arms and never, never let him go.

*I love you,* she told the mound under her maternity dress. *I love you, love you, love you.*

# CHAPTER ELEVEN

THE WEEK PASSED AND SOON it was Friday. Heather wasn't surprised when Karen Boychuk dropped by her classroom about ten minutes after the end-of-the-day bell.

"Looking for your brothers again?" Heather was collecting the children's posters of dried leaves to decorate the town hall. Last week, when the poplar foliage was at its peak of golden perfection, she'd taken the kids out to gather specimens. They'd pressed the leaves dry, then used them to make autumn collages, which were now hanging on the wall at the back of the room. Russ, her self-appointed helper, was going to meet her to help carry them to the hall in about five minutes.

"Yeah. Mom's working again. Can I help you with that?"

"Sure. How about I pull out the tacks, and you pile the posters on my desk?"

They worked together in silence for a couple of minutes.

"So. Any more ideas about applying for university?"

"I'm not sure. I was thinking I might work for a year or two, first."

Heather struggled not to show her dismay. "Why?"

"Well, if Ryan's in school, too, we're going to be really short of money."

Were they planning to live together? It sounded like it. Heather couldn't imagine Karen's parents would be very happy about that, not with Karen so young. "That's what student loans are for, aren't they? Plus, you have all summer to work and save."

"Yeah, but we'll have a lot of expenses. We'll need to buy a car and rent an apartment."

"I thought you were planning to stay with your aunt in Edmonton?"

"Ryan wants to go to the University of Saskatchewan."

Which would mean relocating to Saskatoon not Edmonton. "Have you discussed this with your parents?"

Karen dropped her gaze. "Not yet. They're pretty protective. They really want me to stay with family. I still have a midnight curfew, if you can believe it. Plus, I don't think they like Ryan all that much. Well, they *like* him. But I'm not sure they *trust* him."

She carried the last poster to the desk. "But we'll be nineteen by then," she added, a little defiantly. "We should be able to make up our own minds about what we do."

Heather looked at her sympathetically. She remembered all too well that thirst for independence. Living with an aunt just wasn't the same as being on your own. Still, if money was a factor...

Before she could decide what to say, they were interrupted by a knock at the door. It was Russ, wondering if she was ready to go to the hall. He had his classroom's posters already bundled in his arms.

"I think we're done here. Thanks for helping, Karen."

"Oh, it was fun. I guess I'd better round up my brothers. It was good talking to you, Ms. Collins."

"You, too, Karen." She turned to Russ. They'd decorated the hall together last year and the year before that, too. Another of the bonds of history between them.

"Hang on a minute," she told him. "I need to grab a fresh roll of tape."

T.J. HAD JUST FINISHED A coffee at the café when he saw Heather and Russell Matthew walk across Main Street together. Russ had a bundle of posters in his hands. Heather carried scissors and tape. Vaguely, he recalled Heather mentioning that she would be decorating the hall for the Harvest Festival today.

He hung back, watching his wife and her old friend as they carried on their way. Neither one noticed him. Of course, he was standing almost completely behind a concrete urn of faded summer flowers.

The two chatted easily, happily. He couldn't make out the words, but he could tell by the tone of their voices that it wasn't anything serious. Heather did a lot of laughing, and Russ smiled a lot.

No question those two had always been very compatible. Though they'd been friends forever, and had dated in high school, he couldn't remember ever seeing them argue.

Something he couldn't say about *him* and Heather. She hadn't mentioned the flowers he'd brought for her after their last spat. So, that had been a mistake. Maybe she would have preferred chocolates.

He didn't plan to follow them. Somehow it just happened. Once he reached the corner of Teal Avenue, he found himself taking a left. Russ and Heather were more than a block ahead of him. He followed slowly. When he reached the hall, he took the stairs, pausing after each one, then opened the big door.

His sneakers didn't make a sound on the hardwood floor as he stepped through the foyer. He paused as Russ began to speak.

''Should we hang the posters in the same place as last year?''

T.J. took a step to the right. Now he could see them both, standing left of the stage.

''Sure.'' Heather tucked a strand of her wild hair behind the blue band she was wearing. It matched the denim jumper she had on, faded the same shade of blue as her eyes.

"You know, pregnancy really suits you."

T.J. hung back near the cloak room. He'd been intending to offer to help. He didn't want Heather standing on any chairs, or carrying something heavy.

But he could see that Russ wasn't letting her do any of that, either. He was putting up all the posters. All Heather did was cut tape and hand him one piece at a time.

"Thanks, Russ."

"It makes me wish…" Russ sighed. "Well, it makes me wish things had been different all those years ago. I hate thinking of you going through that first pregnancy alone."

She hadn't been alone—he'd been with her. T.J. clenched his hands, knowing he should either step into the open or slink back outside. Yet he stayed frozen in place, a voyeur to his wife's private conversation with her former lover.

"Russ, you have to stop beating yourself up about that. You didn't know. And it was so many years ago. We've all moved on."

"We have, haven't we?" Russ sounded like he was trying to convince himself. "You're happy with T.J.?"

Why the hell did he have to sound so incredulous? Was it that unbelievable that T.J. could make Heather happy?

"We're adjusting," was the way Heather chose to answer Russ's question. Her response shouldn't have surprised him, but he felt a deep ache in his gut anyway.

Heather tilted her head to one side as she studied the posters Russ had hung. She looked so pretty. The ache traveled up from T.J.'s stomach, lodging in his chest.

"In some ways things are great with T.J. and me."

That would be the sex.

"In others, well, I'm sure you've realized that we married quickly for the sake of the baby."

Did she have to tell him that?

"Yeah, well, marriage can be tricky at times. But when you have kids it's especially important to work things through."

Russ spoke from experience, T.J. guessed. When he and Julie had first moved to Chatsworth they'd had some problems making the adjustment to small-town living. Especially Julie.

"I know you're right, Russ. And I'm sure T.J. and I will be okay."

Oh, heck. She was crying now. Russ noticed shortly after T.J. did. He stepped off the chair, his brow creased with concern. "Heather?"

Dammit. T.J. was not going to stand here and let some other man comfort his wife. Not even if *he* was the reason she was upset in the first place.

"Here you are!" he strode into the hall as if he'd

just arrived. "I saw you on Main Street and thought you might like some help."

Russell backed away from Heather, who quickly swiped a hand over her eyes. "T.J.?" Her voice wobbled a little. "I didn't think you were paying attention when I told you about decorating the hall."

"Well, surprise. I was." He could hardly control his anger. How *dared* Heather complain about their marriage to her old boyfriend? And how dared Russell Matthew even think of touching his wife?

"I'll bet you have lots to do at home," he told Russ now, trying to keep his voice from betraying all that he felt. "I can finish this with Heather."

"Are you sure? I don't mind—"

"I'm sure."

Dead silence followed that. Heather's face flamed with color, but she refused to meet his gaze.

"Okay, then." Russ brushed his hands against his pants. He glanced once at Heather, but she wouldn't look at him, either. "See you tomorrow. Ben's keen to get his hands on one of Lucky's pumpkins. Then he's planning to try creating sidewalk art."

T.J. nodded.

"So, um, good night."

Eventually, finally, Russ left the hall. T.J. waited until he was certain the door had closed. Then he turned to Heather. But before he could say anything, she let loose.

"What in the world is the matter with you? Why did you have to act like such a—such a *caveman?*"

"You're blaming this on me? Tell me, Heather. How do you think I felt when I saw you crying about the sad state of our marriage on your old boyfriend's shoulder?"

"I wasn't crying on his shoulder. We were *talking.*"

"Yeah. About *me.*"

"Not about *you.* About *us.* And I can't help it if I need to talk, T.J. I'm not like you. I can't hold all my feelings inside."

"Well, do you have to unburden yourself on your old lover?"

"I don't think of him that way. He's my friend."

"Right. You think I believe that?" They glared at each other. She was the first to look away. Dammit, she still loved Russell, he knew that she did.

"What do you want from me, T.J.?"

*For you to look at me, just once, the way you look at Russ Matthew.* T.J. blinked, turned away. "Just don't talk about our marriage with him."

"Who should I talk to then?"

"What about me? Your husband."

"That's a laugh. T.J. we can't talk about *anything,* let alone the problems in our marriage."

How many times had Lynn said the exact same thing to him? "Well, I warned you before we got married…"

''Yes, you warned me you wouldn't be the perfect husband. But you didn't tell me you weren't even going to try!'' She tossed the tape at him, then dropped the scissors on the table by the posters. ''Why don't you finish this by yourself? I'm going home.''

THE HARVEST FESTIVAL POTLUCK dinner and dance at the Chatsworth town hall the next day turned out to be a disaster. Heather and T.J. still weren't talking to each other. They'd had one duty dance the whole night long and that was an ordeal.

Heather half expected the same magic that took over whenever they were in the bedroom to descend on them on the dance floor, as well.

But it didn't.

They were awkward together. When he moved in one direction, she went in the other. Several times she stepped on his foot. She became so tense, she couldn't follow the beat of the music anymore.

''Heather, relax.''

''I can't.''

She ended up using her pregnancy as an excuse to leave the party early. T.J. seemed glad to drive her home, even though she'd been willing to walk.

On Sunday she and T.J. by mutual, unspoken, consent, called a truce. They went for dinner at her parent's. That night they made love. Life returned to normal.

A few times Heather caught T.J. taking pictures around town. But he never talked about what he was doing, and she didn't bring up the subject of his daughter, either.

The Saturday after the Harvest Festival, Heather made plans to go shopping in Yorkton with Adrienne. As she drove up to the Jenson's house, Adrienne dashed out the front door. In her haste, she had slipped on a pair of her husband's work boots, and her feet left heavy treads in the white dusting of powder on the sidewalk.

It was snowing, the first storm of the winter. Heather opened her window. The gentle flakes blew in, turning to cold droplets on her skin.

"I'm sorry, Heather. You got here before I could call. Davey just got sick all over the kitchen floor. I'm going to have to cancel the sitter. Ernie's working all day, there's no chance I can get away."

"Oh, poor Davey."

"You mean poor me. Mark my words, it'll be twenty-four hours or less until the next one gets sick. We go through this every year at the beginning of winter." Adrienne looked back at her house as if she didn't want to go in there.

"What can I do to help?" Heather didn't want to risk catching the bug because of the baby. "How about I bring over a lasagna for dinner?"

"That would be great. If I'm lucky, we'll get this

all over within the week. Then maybe we can go shopping next weekend?''

''Or maybe you'll just stay at home and rest,'' Heather predicted. ''Go inside before you get all wet and cold. I'll be back in the afternoon with your dinner. If you need anything else, just phone.''

In the oversize boots, Adrienne trudged back to her house. Heather rolled up her window, then pulled out from the curb. After mentally reviewing the ingredients in her cupboards, she decided she needed to stop at Lucky's before she went home. At the small grocery store she picked out fresh mozzarella cheese, lasagna noodles and mushrooms.

Lucky insisted on carrying her groceries to the car for her.

''Thanks, Lucky.'' She opened the back door so he could load the two paper bags onto the seat.

''No problem. You take care now, Heather. Make sure you put your feet up when you get home. Let that new husband of yours cook you dinner.''

T.J.? Yeah right. He'd probably be at the hardware all day.

Several inches of snow had glazed over the alley by the time Heather returned to Mallard Avenue. She parked in the garage and carried her groceries through the back way, to the kitchen.

The aroma of brewed coffee greeted her. She was surprised to see T.J. at the kitchen table, working on a project of some sort.

Her husband looked equally startled to see her. He spread the weekend paper over the table. Covering— what? Then, noticing her full arms, he jumped out of his chair and took the bags of groceries.

"I thought you were going to Yorkton?"

From his appearance, and the tone of his voice, it was apparent he'd *counted* on her going to Yorkton.

"Davey's sick." Heather moved to the table, ostensibly to get out of his way as he unloaded the groceries. Peeking out from the newspaper camouflage was the corner of a photograph. On the far side of the table she saw the album she'd bought T.J. to give to his daughter.

Why hadn't he wanted her to know what he was doing?

"That's too bad." He opened the fridge and unpacked the cheese, a carton of juice she'd picked up on special.

"I'm going to bake a lasagna and take it over later. Adrienne figures it's just a question of time before her entire household succumbs to the bug."

She turned her back to the table, resisting the urge to snoop further. She crossed the room and removed a package of ground beef from the freezer. "I thought you'd be at the store."

"With this weather—" he glanced out the window into the gray whiteness "—we probably won't be too busy. I think Don will be fine on his own."

They were doing the polite routine. Both talking

about everything but the one subject that was on their minds. Heather longed to ask about the photos and why T.J. had chosen to work on this project on a day when he thought she'd be out of the house.

"Now that your shopping plans are shot, what are you going to do with your day?" T.J.'s eyes darted to the table. She could feel his anxiety. He wanted her out of here.

"Well, I guess I'll take it easy. Read for a few hours, then make that lasagna."

"Maybe you should lie down in the bedroom? That way, if you get tired, you can take a nap."

*God, T.J. Could you be a little more obvious?* Still, she decided to play along with the pretense he was staging. "Sure. I'll do that. A nap might be nice."

He relaxed visibly. "Okay. How about I make some tea and bring it in for you?"

"You're going to make me tea?" That wasn't like T.J. A coffee drinker himself, she doubted he even knew where she kept the tea bags.

"Yeah. I'll make you tea. I can boil water, Heather."

"Oh, I know you can cook, T.J. You're just home so rarely you don't have much of a chance to display your skills."

"Right. Well I'm home now. And I'm going to make you a cup of tea. Is that okay?"

"That's great." She didn't want tea, and she didn't want to lie down and read. She wanted him to show her what he was working on. Fat chance of that.

In the bedroom she changed out of her dressy pants and sweater, into a pair of lounging pants and a sweatshirt. She decided to crawl under the covers to read, since the room was a little chilly. She picked up her latest romance and five minutes later T.J. came in with a mug of peppermint tea and a plate of chocolate-covered biscuits.

"You look cozy."

She tried to appear thoroughly engrossed in her novel. But it was hard to concentrate on a fictional story when she was so curious about what was going on in her own home.

Oh, not that she didn't have a pretty good idea. T.J. was making an album for his daughter.

She wished he would show her. For a second she considered asking.

Instead she forced herself to drink the tea and eat the cookies. She plodded through one chapter and then one more. Then she tried relaxing on the bed, but it was no use.

Sleeping wasn't any easier than reading. She glanced at the clock. It was only two o'clock. She felt like a prisoner in her room. Surely she had every right to go into the kitchen if she wanted. She could start cooking the lasagna.

Mind made up, she went to the kitchen, but T.J. wasn't at the table anymore. The newspaper had been neatly stacked to one side. And there, in the very center of the table, sat the album.

She glanced around the room, as if T.J. might be hiding in one of the corners. "T.J.?" She went to the living room and looked out to the street. Had he quietly slipped outside? Maybe he'd felt compelled to check up on Don Arbuckle at the store.

She returned again to the table, to the album. It had a coil binding and a hard, red cover. T.J. had affixed a label to the front. It simply said, *For Sally*.

Heather paused for a moment, then picked it up. Why shouldn't she look? This had been her idea after all. And T.J. had left the book on the table. If he hadn't wanted her to see it, surely he would have tucked it away somewhere.

She opened the album at random and came across the cookie-baking photos. T.J. had made a little story out of the pictures, adding captions under each photo. "Tastes good!" he'd put under the one where he was taking a bite from the freshly made cookie.

Under the first one of her, he'd printed, "Heather— my new wife. You'll like her. She smiles a lot. And makes good cookies."

Heather put a hand to her face. Closed her eyes.

"So what do you think?"

T.J.'s voice startled her. She opened her eyes and saw him standing in the kitchen, a laundry basket in his hands. He'd been in the basement.

"I didn't know you were still in the house. I thought maybe you'd gone to the store."

She couldn't tell if he was angry she'd looked through his album. He seemed pretty calm. She flipped back to the beginning page. The very first picture was of his parents' home. "This is where I grew up," he'd printed.

Then a photo of the store. "My father opened this store almost fifty years ago. Now I work here."

"I know Sally can't read, yet," he said. "But I thought maybe Lynn—"

There was something vulnerable on his face, something that tugged at Heather's heart. It took a real effort not to cry.

"I'm sure Lynn will read this to her." She couldn't imagine a mother denying her child this glimpse into her father's world. "It's wonderful, T.J."

"Just a bunch of pictures. Nothing special."

Did he really think that? The time he'd taken putting this together belied his words. "I'm just so glad that you did this." She brushed her fingers gently over the pages as she went back through each one. T.J.'s photos of the lake, and the school, of Lucky standing in front of his grocery store under the green-and-white striped awning, of Donna Werner holding a pot of coffee as if it was an extension of her arm, all brought Chatsworth vividly to life.

T.J. had a good eye. And an interesting sense of

composition. Even though they'd been taken with a cheap disposable, the pictures were very nice.

"You have hidden talents. I never would have imagined you'd be such a great photographer."

"Well, I had fun. But I doubt if these pictures will mean anything to Sally. Just a bunch of people she's never met. Places she's never seen."

"It'll mean something. Because you're her dad."

She lost him then. The exact second the words were out of her mouth, she saw his eyes turn cold, his entire body stiffen.

"I may be her biological father. But Sally already has a dad."

Heather knew there'd be no point arguing. But T.J. was wrong. He and Sally had a connection. Damaged, yes, but still a connection. The sooner he moved to repair it, the better off they'd all be.

# CHAPTER TWELVE

T.J.'S APPOINTMENT WAS FOR TWO o'clock. He drove to Yorkton in plenty of time, anxious to get through the initial interview and be home before Heather finished school at three-thirty.

Maurice Waters's office was on a quiet commercial side street, above a drug store that looked as though it had been in business for about a hundred years.

The stairs to the second story were steep and shallow. The brown, indoor-outdoor carpeting was worn at the center of the treads. At the top of the stairs three doors led off from a small hallway.

T.J. had been here before, more than a year ago. He'd hired Maurice Waters to go to Toronto and make sure his daughter was happy. Today he was at the private investigator's office for Heather's sake.

Although he couldn't find the words to admit it, her idea of taking those pictures and making that album had been pretty clever. He'd posted the package earlier this week and had no idea how Sally and Lynn were going to react when they received it.

But he felt so much better. It was unbelievable. He

was sleeping more restfully at night. Finding it easier to talk to Heather without turning every conversation into a sparring match.

No, he wasn't the perfect husband, he would never be that, but some pressure inside him had eased a little.

He wanted to do something for Heather, too. Not just buy her a gift or take her out for dinner. He wanted to do something special. Something that proved he understood her, the way she obviously understood him. It had taken him a long time to figure out what that could be.

After tapping on the door twice, with no reply, T.J. tried the doorknob. It turned and the door opened easily.

Maurice was in his forties, average build, a little pudgy. He sat at the lone desk in the room, focused on his computer. He had a pair of earphones on, which explained why he hadn't heard the knocking.

The room was crowded with bookshelves and several long tables. Scattered throughout were files and papers. In one corner, a photocopier hummed. T.J. also spotted a scanner, a fax machine and a sleek laser printer.

Finally Maurice noticed him. He whipped off his earphones, stood up and offered a hand. ''Good— you made it. How have you been, T.J.? Take that chair right there.'' Maurice indicated a cheap folding chair—the only piece of furniture in the place that didn't have anything on it.

T.J. gingerly settled his weight on the small chair. "I'm well, thanks. Got married recently—don't know if you heard."

Maurice offered his congratulations, then turned quickly to business. "You said this was a delicate matter?"

"I want you to find someone."

"I do that sort of work all the time. And who is it that you would like to locate?"

T.J. hesitated a second. Told himself he was doing the right thing. Took a deep breath.

"I want you to find a baby that was given up for adoption about fifteen years ago. My wife was his mother."

HALLOWEEN CAME AND WENT. Heather had a party for her class, then spent the evening handing out treats at the front door and trying to recognize the kids behind the costumes.

Then it was November. The leaves were long gone from the trees, and snow accumulated from one storm to the next. She gained weight steadily and her health remained good. The baby was becoming more and more real to her. She worked at compiling a list of names, but could rarely interest T.J. in a discussion of the subject.

He had softened noticeably since the day he'd

mailed off that album, but he was still holding back where his relationship with her—and their unborn baby—was concerned.

Meanwhile, despite the winter, progress on the Matthews' house remained steady. The workers were painting the interior now. After that they would be installing bathroom and kitchen counters, cabinets and flooring. It seemed the Matthews would be in their home by Christmas, as planned.

Heather imagined the four of them sipping hot chocolate around the Christmas tree—it would be beautiful, Julie would make sure of that. There would be carols in the background and the kids would both be dressed like ads for the GAP. Russ, unlike T.J., would laugh a lot. He'd make silly jokes that would set Ben giggling. He'd tickle his daughter, then hold her close in his arms.

*Oh, stop it, Heather!* Ever since Russ and Julie had moved back to Chatsworth, she'd been driving herself crazy picturing their perfect life together. It seemed she couldn't help but compare her life the way it was now, to how it could have been if she and Russell…

*No.* She couldn't keep doing this.

It wasn't right for her to envy another family their happiness. Besides, didn't she have her own blessings to be grateful for this year?

She had only six weeks of teaching left until Christmas holidays when she would begin her one-year maternity leave. Next Christmas, *she* would have a little one to sit by the Christmas tree with. Somehow inserting T.J. in the picture wasn't as easy. When she finally managed it, he sat stubbornly in one corner, his mouth set in a scowl.

Heather rubbed her eyes. The day had felt long. She gathered the resource material she needed to prepare for the next day of class, then quickly wiped down the boards.

As she completed her tasks, she thought about Karen Boychuk. She hadn't been around recently. Probably she was busy keeping up her school work and looking after her brothers. Ryan Farrell would take up whatever time was left over. Not too much time, though, Heather hoped.

She was glad Karen had an exciting relationship with a boy she really liked. But Heather was concerned Karen might be willing to sacrifice her education for Ryan's. And that, Heather was convinced, would be a mistake. Even if Karen and Ryan did end up spending the rest of their lives together, it would still be a mistake.

The next day at school, Heather tried asking one of the twins about their sister. "Is Karen all right? I haven't seen her lately."

"She's okay." Perry said.

Right away Heather realized she'd asked the wrong brother. She'd mixed them up thanks to a change in seating order. She wouldn't get more than those two words out of Perry.

The day passed and she never did find the right moment to question Paul. But fortunately, Karen picked that day to stop by again.

"I've missed seeing you, Karen. How are you doing?"

The young woman was in a short sheepskin jacket, jeans and boots with heels that surely couldn't contend with real snow and ice.

"Not bad." Karen sighed and sank onto one of the desktops in the front row.

"Are the boys outside?"

"No. They took the bus home. I just wanted to…talk."

Heather tidied up her desk, giving Karen time to gather her thoughts. And perhaps some courage, as well. The young woman's face was extremely pale, her expression drawn. Had she and Ryan fought?

"Ms. Collins, how did you know when you were pregnant?"

Thud. Heather bent to retrieve the stapler she'd dropped to the floor. *Oh, my God,* she wanted to scream. But she focused on speaking calmly. "Well, my breasts were tender. And I was very tired. Of course I skipped my period—that's the most reliable sign."

Karen swung her feet to and fro, keeping her gaze on the tips of her boots.

Tentatively Heather began to probe. "Have you missed your period, Karen?"

She sniffed. Then nodded. "Twice."

Oh, no. *Oh, no.* Heather came round the desk and took Karen's hands. "Have you been to the doctor?"

"Not yet."

"Taken a test?"

"I'm afraid to buy the kit."

"So you haven't talked to your parents?"

"I can't do that."

She burst into tears then and Heather saw nothing to do but to pull her into a hug. She squelched the impulse to tell the young woman it would be all right.

It wouldn't be all right. Not if Karen truly was pregnant.

No matter what turn she took at this stage, great difficulties were ahead. No one knew this better than Heather.

"Karen, have you talked to Ryan?"

"No one. I've told no one. Only you."

Oh, boy, this was going to be tricky. "Well, I'm glad you've told me. This is an awful burden to carry by yourself." Her first impulse was to ask about birth control. Why they hadn't been using it. Or what had gone wrong if they had.

But what was the purpose in making Karen feel bad at this point? Besides, Heather knew, only too well, how unimportant something like a condom could seem when you were with a man you thought was the love of your life. She'd only made that mistake with Russ once, but once had been enough.

"What am I going to do, Ms. Collins? What in the world am I going to do?"

"Well, you do have a few choices." And none of them were easy. "But first you need to confirm this pregnancy. Make an appointment with your doctor. Since you're eighteen you can do this without your mother."

Karen nodded. "I brought the doctor's number with me. Do you think I could go to your house to make the call? I can never be sure of privacy at home."

T.J. wouldn't be leaving the store for hours.

"That's a good idea. Dry your eyes." She handed her a tissue from the box on her desk. "That's a girl. We'll take this one step at a time."

After they confirmed the pregnancy, then she would have to convince Karen to speak to her parents. And to Ryan.

Neither conversation would be easy.

Oh, Lord. A part of Heather wished Karen had chosen to lay this problem on someone else's shoulders. She didn't want to go through this again. Her first pregnancy had marked the worst period of her life. She wanted only to forget.

And yet, in all these years, she'd never managed to do that. So maybe it was providence that she was here now for Karen. At any rate, no matter how she felt about the situation, she was committed.

Karen had trusted her. She couldn't let her down.

AT TWO IN THE MORNING, Heather woke from a restless sleep, heart pounding, stomach in knots. She'd had such an awful dream.... It came back in a flash. She was *pregnant*.

*Oh, no! This can't be, this can't be.* She put a hand to her stomach, felt the bulge. *No, no, please, God, no.*

She opened her eyes, saw the unfamiliar shadows of a different bedroom than the one she expected. Full consciousness returned and she gradually relaxed. She wasn't a student anymore, nor unmarried and alone. Yes, she was pregnant, but she was thirty-five this time, she had a husband, she *wanted* this baby.

Resting her hands on her abdomen, she took several deep breaths as her body slowly turned off the panic mode. Eventually, she levered her body to the side and gazed at her husband's form sprawled out next to her.

Because she was always so tired, she was rarely awake while T.J. slept. She enjoyed the rare opportunity to examine him when his guard was down. He was on his side. Relaxed, his mouth formed a gentle smile. His forehead was smooth and untroubled.

His presence beside her provided further reassurance. Still, she didn't think she could fall back to sleep quite yet. A mug of warm milk seemed like a good idea. At the very least, the extra calcium would be good for the baby.

Heather slipped out from the covers, tucking her feet into slippers and her arms into a velour robe. As she made her way to the kitchen, she cinched the belt at her expanding waistline.

Her recurring dream dated back to her first pregnancy, but she hadn't had it since her marriage to Nick. Undoubtedly the old demons had been awakened by Karen's announcement this afternoon.

In the kitchen, she turned on the light over the stove, then filled a mug with milk, and stuck it in the microwave for a minute. While she waited, she gazed out at the snow-covered trees in her yard. They looked like giant snowmen after the latest dump. And it was still coming now, the gentle powder catching glints of light from the streetlights.

She wondered if Karen was sleeping right now, or if nightmares were troubling her, too. Poor Karen. Heather felt so badly for her. She remembered the churning emotions of those first months.

She'd been embarrassed at being pregnant so young—actually ashamed, even though she didn't really think she'd done anything that terrible. Though he wasn't her boyfriend at the time, she'd been so in love with Russell.

Still there was a stigma attached to being an unwed mother and she'd felt sorry for the disappointment she knew she would bring to her parents.

Some days she'd almost drowned in her fear—about the upcoming labor, about her future and that of her child. Other days all she'd felt was anger. Why had this happened to her? It wasn't fair. Usually—usually!—she was so very careful.

What a frightening, tumultuous, overwhelming experience that pregnancy had been. And now Karen was going through the same thing, her thoughts probably traveling down the same, fruitless lines that Heather's once had.

Why wasn't I more careful? It was only the one time. If I could only have another chance...

But pregnancy was a hard fact that didn't allow for second chances.

What would Karen decide to do in the end? Heather took her warmed milk to the living room where she settled on a chair near the window. Would Karen choose abortion? Would she keep her child? Or have the baby then give it up for adoption?

Heather had never really considered abortion, even though it had seemed at the time—perhaps mistakenly—that terminating the pregnancy would be the easiest route. But in the end, because the child was Russell's and she'd loved him so much, she'd been unable to simply dispose of the baby inside of her.

At first she'd dreamed that she and Russ would reconcile. They'd marry and raise the child together.

Though she'd heard he was dating someone new in Vancouver, she didn't worry. Not at first. He'd always been open about the fact that he went out with other girls when he was away. That had been their agreement, though she herself had never wanted to see any guy but him.

She'd waited for him to phone—generally she heard from him at least once a month, if not more. But that term he didn't call. She was upset, but decided that telling him about the pregnancy in person would be better, anyway. She'd wait for Christmas when they would both be in Chatsworth with their families. But for the first time Russ didn't come home for the holidays at the end of term. His mother told her he'd been invited to spend the season with his new girlfriend's family.

Mrs. Matthew hadn't been pleased. This new girlfriend presented a distinct threat to Betty Matthew's plans for her son. She wanted him to marry Heather and spend the rest of his days raising a family in Chatsworth.

If Mrs. Matthew had been aware of Heather's pregnancy, perhaps things would have worked out differently. But Heather had been diligent about keeping her secret.

And so Christmas had passed, and then January, and despite Betty Matthew's hopes, and Heather's own deepest desires, the option of marrying Russ had faded into an impossibility. In her final months of pregnancy, Heather vacillated between her two remaining choices—keeping the baby and being a single mom, or giving the child up for adoption.

She'd gone for counseling. She'd talked to her parents, to her minister, to her doctor. She'd prayed.

And finally, as if in answer to those prayers, Heather heard about a couple who'd been on the list for a baby for five years. The father was a doctor. The woman was prepared to stay home full-time to raise a child.

Everything about these people had sounded so perfect, she felt like she no longer faced a decision at all. Obviously this couple had much more to offer a baby than she did. And so she signed the papers and told herself she was doing the right thing. She'd gone back to school, obtained her teaching degree, eventually married Nick and dreamed about having her own family.

But then Nick had been killed...

Heather finished the last of her milk. Her stupid dream had brought back all these memories—at a time in her life when she'd been determined not to dwell on the mistakes of the past.

What would it take to make her let them go? Or was she going to be stuck with these ghosts forever?

## CHAPTER THIRTEEN

AFTER WORK THE NEXT DAY, Heather stopped at the post office to pick up the mail. She paused when she saw a padded envelope with a Toronto return address from Sally Collins.

Heather smiled, then tucked the envelope with the rest of the mail into her leather bag. As she left the post office, she was tempted to run over to the Handy Hardware to show T.J. his package.

But instantly she realized that was a bad idea. T.J. would want to be alone when he saw this. He'd need to prepare himself. Knowing him, he would anticipate the worst—that Lynn was returning his album with a note asking him not to contact Sally again.

That's the way T.J.'s mind seemed to work, always dwelling on the negative. But from things her mother had said, Heather knew that T.J.'s parents thought Lynn was a fine person and an excellent mother. Surely she would want her child to know her father.

Heather returned home and prepared an easy dinner of steak and salad. For once, T.J. came home shortly after six. She heard the door open, his steps down the hall.

"T.J.?" She met him in the entrance to the kitchen. As always, her husband's appearance gave her a physical thrill she couldn't ignore. His dark hair had grown a bit long, and she loved the way it curled on his forehead and around his ears.

"How are you doing?" His gaze settled on her growing middle. She wished he'd touch her there, but he rarely did. Occasionally, after they made love, he would rest his hand briefly on her stomach. But she got the impression he was never really comfortable focusing on her pregnancy.

"I'm fine."

"You look—excited. Did you win the lottery?"

A flash of amusement lit his eyes and again she had to catch her breath. Her husband was especially handsome when he smiled.

"Something came in the mail." She was so keyed up, she could hardly keep herself from running to open it herself.

"A rebate on the electrical bill?" he teased.

"A package from *Toronto*."

"Oh." His eyes widened, his expression turned serious. He understood right away what this had to be.

He hung his jacket in the closet, his face suddenly so blank she wondered if he hadn't heard her. After he'd removed his shoes, he didn't come into the kitchen, as usual, but turned down the hall.

She didn't follow, much as she longed to, but instead went to the fridge to pull out the chilling bottle of white wine. She had no intention of letting this occasion slip by without a little celebration, even though she couldn't drink herself.

She uncorked the bottle, tossed the salad, finished the steaks on the grill. Fifteen minutes passed with no sign of T.J.

Finally, she could no longer stand the waiting.

"T.J.?" She moved toward their bedroom. "T.J.?" she whispered again. "Are you okay?"

Had she been wrong to assume good news?

She paused at the open doorway. T.J. sat on the bed, his back to her. He must have heard her call out to him, but he didn't respond.

Heather considered leaving. But what if he truly was in pain? She didn't want him stewing alone. Tentatively she stepped into the room and made her way to his side. She placed a hand on his shoulder. He lifted his head to look at her. He had tears in his eyes.

"She's grown. A lot."

"Oh, T.J."

On his lap was an album. Not his own, but one his daughter had made. Heather glimpsed a skewed picture of a funny-looking doll; an out-of-focus shot of a scraggly pup; a third one of a child much older than the one in the photo in T.J.'s wallet. She was riding a tricycle through a pile of gold and red leaves, smiling triumphantly toward the camera.

"She's just like you!" The resemblance was amazing.

T.J. handed her several sheets of stationery. It was a letter from Lynn. Did he want her to read this? She glanced back at him, her brows raised. He nodded his approval.

Lynn had neat handwriting.

T.J., that photo album was inspired. I would never have believed you were capable of a gesture like that. So you've changed. I wonder why...but more on that later.

Sally is so excited. I wish you could see the way she's been showing the album to everyone, bragging about her Chatsworth daddy (I hope you don't mind that we call you that). I also hope you enjoy the album we put together for you. As you'll be able to tell, Sally took most of these pictures herself. I'm sorry so many of them are of her new puppy and her doll, but those are her favorite things right now.

T.J., I know we've had our difficulties. At first, I have to admit I thought Sally was better off without you in her life. But seeing the way she reacted to your pictures, well, I believe I may have been wrong. You are her father, and she really does need you. She asks me every day when she can see you.

Rather than you coming to Toronto again, though, I think it might be better if Sally came to you. She's too young to fly alone, so I would bring her. Do you think spring break would work? Unfortunately we've already made plans for Christmas, but maybe next year, she could spend part of those holidays with you, too.

I see from your pictures that you've married again. (Is this the girl who changed you, I wonder?) I'm glad about that. I can tell she's a lovely person, just from the sparkle in her eyes.

Take care, T.J. I'd tell you not to work too hard, but I wouldn't want to start another fight (ha, ha).

Talk to you soon,

Lynn

It was almost too much for Heather to take in. The important thing, she reminded herself, was that Lynn was willing to bring Sally for a visit.

"Isn't that wonderful, T.J.? It'll be so great to have your daughter for a visit." Heather couldn't wait to meet her. She didn't doubt that she and Sally would get along. She was good with kids. And Sally was young enough that she shouldn't be resentful.

The visit would be good for Sally. She'd see where her father came from and get to know her grandparents. But she'd spend most of her time with her dad—Heather would see to that. It was important for Sally. And perhaps even more important for T.J.

"I can't believe she wants to see me."

Heather took his hand, squeezing it between both of hers. If T.J. could only let himself, he'd be a fine father. "We'll make sure Sally has a wonderful time in Chatsworth."

"I don't know, Heather. What if she ends up disappointed? If I let her down—"

"You won't." Heather tried to sound confident. But she actually wasn't. T.J. had done such a good job of convincing himself he was a lousy husband and father, that he just couldn't seem to break out of the pattern he'd set for himself.

She wanted to help. But how? If Sally's pictures didn't show him the way, what else could?

Heather glanced down at the letter in her hand. She wondered about those last paragraphs Lynn had written.

Heather folded the pages and returned them to the envelope. She snuck a close look at her husband's face. He was still focused on the album, studying the pictures in minute detail, as if searching for a clue.

*Is this the girl who changed you,* Lynn had asked. But had Heather really changed him? At heart T.J. was the same impish boy who'd been so miserable to her when she was a kid. *What do you wash your hair with? Carrot juice?*

As a teacher she heard boys make those sorts of comments every day. Usually to a girl they had a secret crush on...

Was it possible that T.J.—? But, no, she couldn't believe he'd ever liked her, wanted to go out with her.

*Why not? He made love with you, didn't he?*

Yes, but T.J. had probably made love with a good many Chatsworth girls. She'd just been convenient—

*Yeah, when you were pregnant in Saskatoon and he used to hang around all the time. You think it was because of your beautiful pregnant "glow"?*

Okay, there were those months to contend with. He'd been a friend—and the one night, more than a friend. Surely most guys wouldn't find a woman who was seven months pregnant very appealing. Unless they had special feelings for her...?

She wished she could just ask him. But knowing T.J., he wouldn't tell her how he really felt anyway. He'd say he thought she was sexy. He'd refuse to dig any deeper than that. If, indeed, there was any place deeper to dig.

T.J. WAS GETTING USED TO THE idea that he might have a role in his daughter's life, after all. He'd actually phoned Sally one night. That hadn't gone too well. The little girl was cranky—he'd forgotten about the two-hour time difference and called at bedtime— and he wasn't sure she even understood who he was.

But he tried not to be discouraged. He was just a bit rusty at this father thing.

He needed practice.

He started talking to the preschool kids when they came in with their parents to the hardware. He learned what made them laugh, what to do when they were shy. He found out which toys they were interested in, then used that information to send Sally a gift for her birthday—a stuffed animal fashioned after a character in a popular children's TV show.

She phoned him to say she liked it.

He felt like dancing. She liked his present. Somehow, he'd gotten something right, all on his own.

That success, small as it was, got him wondering if there might be hope for his relationship with Heather. He was still waiting for word on her son. She'd helped him establish a relationship, however fragile, with his daughter. It seemed only right that he do something of equal magnitude for her.

When he finally got the word from Maurice, he was as excited as a school kid. He left work early that day. Set the manila envelope on the kitchen table. And waited.

# CHAPTER FOURTEEN

"WHY DID YOU DO THIS?" Heather's face was so pale, her freckles stood out like oddly shaped polka dots.

T.J. was tempted to make a wisecrack, but managed to restrain himself. Old habits died hard.

"I thought—" How to put this? "I thought it would make you happy."

"Isn't that so like a man? You know Nick used to think every problem could be solved with action, too."

He frowned. What did her first husband have to do with this?

"Shortly after we were married, he offered to try and find my son for me, too. At least he *asked* first."

Her anger, mixed with resentment, had T.J. backing away from the kitchen table where Heather was now standing. He'd told her the envelope contained information on her son, but she hadn't even opened it. "I just wanted to help."

"This isn't going to help anything." She tossed the envelope onto the table.

He'd never seen her so angry before. Redheads

were infamous for their terrible tempers. Not Heather. She was an even-keeled person under the most trying of circumstances.

"But I thought if you could be reassured that he was happy…" T.J. had glanced at the report first, not wanting to land his wife with any unsettling surprises. Everything Mr. Waters had managed to find out about the boy and his family had been glowingly positive.

"I did what I could do to assure my son's happiness on the day he was born." Heather's eyes were enormous and shining with unshed tears. "I entrusted his care to a wonderful set of parents."

T.J. swallowed. He'd never before appreciated how tough that must have been for her. He thought back to the day Sally had been born. Holding her in his arms, he'd felt a flood of love and responsibility. Heather must have felt those same things for her child. Probably even more.

And yet, she'd let him go…

"T.J., no matter what's in this damn report about my son, it won't be enough. Do you understand? No amount of words on a page could ever be enough. If I know his address, I'll want to see him. If I see him, I'll want to touch him. Can't you see how impossible it all is?"

She was so upset, it hurt to watch her.

"Sit down, Heather." He wished he could put his arms around her, but they never embraced, except when they were headed for the bedroom. He pulled out a chair, but she ignored it.

"You had no right to go behind my back and do this. No right at all." Her voice shook as she said this. She crossed her arms under her breasts as if holding herself together.

T.J. gave up trying to defend himself. Obviously he'd made a serious miscalculation. He should have known better than to trust his instincts.

"Look, if I made a mistake, I'm sorry. Okay?" His apology came out sounding belligerent. He shook his head, wondering why it was so hard to make his words and actions match his feelings. He *was* sorry. He'd wanted to make her happy, to have her glow with gladness and relief. Instead she was so worked up, he worried for her health.

"Let me make you some tea."

"I don't want any *tea*. I think I'm going to— I'm going to go for a walk." She glanced out the window uncertainly. A storm had blown in that afternoon. The wind was howling and the snow was already several inches deep on the sidewalk he'd shoveled just an hour ago.

"Heather, don't go out in the blizzard. Please. If you need some space, I'll go back to work for a few hours."

"Oh, wouldn't you just love that. An excuse to hide out at the hardware store and avoid me for another evening."

Where was this coming from? She'd never complained about his work hours before. In fact, he'd assumed his long days suited her, allowing her to maintain a bit of her old privacy and freedom. After all, the only reason she'd married him was because she was pregnant. He never forgot that. Not one minute of one day.

"Tell me what you want." He leaned back against the kitchen counter, suddenly exhausted. This had turned into one hell of a disaster. "Do you want to be alone? Do you want company?"

"I told you. I want to go for a walk." Stubbornly, she went to the hall closet and pulled on a long wool coat she'd borrowed from Adrienne, mitts, a hat. Next, she slipped her feet into a pair of well-gripped winter boots.

"This is crazy. Look out that window. Please stay home."

"I'm going to Adrienne's," she announced calmly. "I'll be back before nine." Then she opened the door and blew away on a gust of cold, Artic wind.

HEATHER BATTLED THE WIND and thick snow outside. She welcomed the icy cold on her cheeks, the freezing air that made her catch her breath and dig her mittens into the lined pockets of the coat that Adrienne had worn for all three of her pregnancies.

She knew T.J.'s motivations had been good, but that only made the whole situation harder.

How many times had she been tempted to try and find her baby? More than she could ever count. But she'd always felt that such a move would be selfish on her part.

Her baby was fifteen years old now. Ironically, just a few years older than Russ and Julie's son, Ben. She knew Ben's presence in Chatsworth hadn't helped her any. She couldn't seem to look at the boy and not think about his half brother, living somewhere in Saskatoon, just four hours north of here.

A sob burst out—it felt as though it had come straight from her heart. Heather didn't try to hold it back. No one was out on an evening like this and even if they were the howling wind would drown out any sound. And the dumping of snow would explain any moisture on her cheeks when she arrived at Adrienne's.

Her son. Her son. She didn't think it was healthy, but she still thought of him. She imagined him having the late growth spurt that had seen Russell shoot up above all his classmates the year before he'd turned fifteen.

He'd be growing up. Like most kids his age, his world would begin to revolve around his peer group now. A steady family life would help ground him.

The unexpected appearance of his birth mother, however, might very well send him into a tailspin.

Heather had read enough accounts of reunions between birth mothers and their children to know that this could happen.

It was better, from a child's perspective, if such a reunion occurred on their own initiative.

Heather had made it clear to the agency that had handled the adoption that if ever her son wanted to find her, they were to let her know. But until that day, she wasn't going to rock his world just to make herself feel better.

Heather stopped short. Already she was in front of the Jensons' house—nothing in Chatsworth was farther than a few blocks away. Cheerful lights blazed from all the windows in the house. Ernie's truck was parked in the drive, behind Adrienne's station wagon.

She pulled off a mitten so she could check the time. Adrienne was probably preparing supper. This was a very inconvenient time. Heather glanced over her shoulder toward her own home, then resolutely turned back to the Jensons'.

She couldn't go back to T.J. Not yet.

She waded through snow drifts to the side door where she pulled open the screen, then knocked. After a couple of seconds with no response, she opened the unlocked door and stepped inside.

A mound of boots in assorted sizes were piled on either side of the entry. Snow pants, mittens, toques and scarves were in another heap.

"Adrienne?"

She could smell a spicy tomato sauce, heard a TV program, kids yelling.

"Adrienne?" She tried calling louder.

"Heather, is that you?" Adrienne came out of the kitchen drying her hands on a towel. Her hair was gathered in a loose knot on the top of her head. She wore a shirt of brilliant jewel colors that trailed over a pair of faded jeans.

"I know this is a crazy time." Heather brushed the melting snowflakes—or were they tears?—from her face.

"No crazier than any other. I've just put supper on the table." She turned to the hall and hollered, "Okay, turn off that TV. Wash your hands and come and eat."

Ernie was first in the room. His hair was rumpled, his shirt untucked. She could tell by the tired lines in his face that he'd just finished a long shift. But he took Heather's unexpected appearance in stride. "Want me to set another plate, Addie?"

"No." Heather backed up a step. "I don't want to interrupt." And yet she'd shown up unannounced at the family dinner hour. She realized she wasn't making any sense.

"I just—I had cabin fever and needed to get out for a walk. Now I'll turn back and head home before T.J. starts to worry."

Adrienne frowned. "What's—?" She looked at

her friend's face carefully, then tossed the tea towel in her hands onto the chair. "We're going to the café for a few minutes, Ernie. You supervise dinner here, and Davey, help your dad with the dishes when you're done."

"But, Mom. I have lots of homework tonight."

"Great. That means no more TV until it's done."

Heather had to smile at Adrienne's no-nonsense manner of dealing with her kids. Of course, with three boys, she'd had to learn early how to maintain the upper hand.

"That's fine, Addie. Take your time." Ernie seemed unperturbed by the prospect of his wife dashing out at the dinner hour. He was such a steady guy. The perfect foil for creative, impulsive Adrienne.

Adrienne donned her own winter gear and a few minutes later the two women were outside. Already so much snow had fallen that the sidewalks were impassable. Heather and Adrienne marched down the middle of the road together, following tracks made recently by a big truck. The blistering wind and buffeting snow rendered conversation impossible. They both waited to talk until they had shut the café door behind them.

"Wow, what a night!" Adrienne brushed snow off herself and stomped her feet on the mat. The café was almost empty. Only one elderly couple sat at a table near the window.

Heather waved at them, then moved to the back. Adrienne followed.

"So what gives?" she asked in a low voice once they were seated.

"It's T.J.," she confessed. "You won't believe what he's done now."

"Not again." Adrienne signaled Donna Werner, who'd just peeked out from the kitchen. Adrienne held up an empty coffee mug.

Donna nodded, then came round with two pots, one filled with hot water. "Terrible storm, isn't it? Supposed to break by the morning though. Herbal tea, Heather?"

"Thanks. That would be nice."

"Bring us a couple hamburgers, too, please," Adrienne decided, without any consultation. When Heather raised her eyebrows, Adrienne just shrugged. "You've got to feed that baby, and I'm missing my supper."

"I'm sorry about that, Adrienne. I was just so...*angry.* I had to get out of that house and I didn't know where else to go."

"Hey, it happens." Adrienne didn't look put out. "Once I took off after a big fight—about what I have *no* idea—intending to drive out to my cousin's farm. Thought I'd have a nice, long pout, only I backed the wagon into a snowdrift in my own alley. Had to call Ernie to help shovel me out."

Heather smiled. "It's nice to know you and Ernie fight sometimes. You seem so perfect together."

"Heather, every couple fights, or else something really is wrong. You and T.J. were always striking sparks against each other. No reason to think marriage would change that."

"But he's just so distant. It drives me crazy. Today he told me he thought I liked it when he worked late because it kept him out of my hair. Why would he think a crazy thing like that?"

Adrienne tapped her temple, indicating that she thought her friend was being simple. "Maybe he thinks the same thing you do. That you only married him because of the baby."

Heather rolled her eyes. "That doesn't mean we can't try and build a relationship together. Half the couples in this town got married because they were in the exact same predicament."

Adrienne nodded. "Chad and Bernie for one."

"Exactly. And look how happy they are now."

"Well, you and T.J. can be happy, too."

"I thought so at first. Now I'm not sure." Heather checked her tea and when she found it wasn't too hot, took a sip.

"Why do you say that?"

"Every time I hope we're headed in the right direction, something happens and I think I can't possibly live with this man."

"So what happened this time?"

Heather made sure her voice was low. "He hired a private investigator to locate my first baby."

"No."

"Without even consulting me. He brought home the report today and had the nerve to think I'd be *pleased.* Of course, I won't look at the thing. I can't."

"I understand." Adrienne patted her hand.

Almost as much as the invasion of her privacy, Heather was bothered by the secrecy with which T.J. had gone about this. She hadn't had a clue. Which made her wonder what other secrets her husband might be keeping.

Like the embezzlement of his ex-law firm's trust account funds?

No. Angry as she was at T.J., she didn't believe he could stoop that low.

But where did all his money come from? She'd seen a few of his monthly investment statements lying around. She hadn't meant to snoop, but when she'd found a stack on the kitchen table, her eye had been drawn to the bottom line. He had several hundred thousand in retirement funds. And more than double that amount in stocks and bonds. She *knew* he wasn't pulling in that kind of money from the hardware store.

"I never have any idea what T.J.'s thinking."

"With men, sometimes I think it's better that you

don't know,'' Adrienne said. ''Usually it's only about food, sports or sex, anyway.''

''Yeah? I wonder which of those three T.J. is thinking about right now.''

''If he knows what's good for him, it won't be sex.''

## CHAPTER FIFTEEN

WHEN HEATHER CAME HOME about an hour later, she found T.J. in the living room, sitting in an armchair in the dark.

What was he doing? Serving penance?

"It's okay, T.J." She hung up her coat, wearily. "I know your intentions were good." She kicked off her boots, then went to sit across from him on the sofa.

He stared back at her for a long time. What was up with him? "Is something wrong?"

"Why are you asking me? You're the one who gets to decide what's right and what's wrong in this relationship, aren't you?"

He was *angry*. Heather couldn't believe it. She'd come home prepared to be magnanimous, prepared to forgive him for that terrible breach of her privacy. And now *this?*

"What are you talking about?"

"I'm talking about our relationship. Such as it is," he muttered.

She noticed he had a half-empty beer in his hand. Had there been others?

He followed the direction of her gaze and raised the can in mocking salute. "This is number three, Heather. Since you're obviously counting."

"Well, if you're drunk…" She half rose from her seat, more upset than she was letting on.

"Sit down."

He spoke so forcibly, she did as he said, without question.

"T.J., you're beginning to scare me."

"Don't be a fool. I'm not drunk and I'm certainly not going to hurt you. I figure it's report card time for our marriage. So what do you think, Heather? Would you give us a passing grade so far? A C minus, maybe? Or perhaps a D?"

"What do *you* think?" she countered.

"Why ask me? You're the one whose opinion counts."

"Would you stop with all this badgering and just tell me what's bothering you?"

"Yeah, I'll tell you. I'm sick of the double standard around here. You think my relationship with Sally needs work, so you give me a couple of cameras and a photo album. Now, I'm not saying you weren't right, but when I try to do the same for you—"

"You can't mean to suggest our situations are similar?"

"They're not as different as you think."

"They're *completely* different."

"Come on, Heather. You're stuck in the past. You've never gotten over what happened between you and Russ."

"I *gave up* my baby. Excuse me if I've had a hard time getting over that."

T.J. shook his head. She'd never seen his expression so bleak, his mouth so hard.

"I'm not talking about the baby, Heather. He's just the excuse. It's Russ you can't get over. In fact, I don't think you're even willing to try."

HEATHER LOOKED AS SHOCKED as if he'd struck her. "How can you say that? Do you think I'm the kind of person who would love another woman's husband?"

"I wasn't suggesting you acted on your feelings. But you do have them. Don't try to deny it. I've seen the way you look at him. You're obsessed with the new house he's building. Tell me you don't fantasize about moving in—"

"Stop! I can't stand to hear you talk that way."

"You can't stand the truth, you mean."

She glowered at him. "You want the truth? Okay, I admit I have many fond memories of Russ. I'll even admit I consider him something of an ideal husband and father. That doesn't mean I'm still in love with him."

She paused, expecting T.J. to go on the offensive again. But he surprised her by merely shaking his head and withdrawing to the basement. To watch TV? Lift weights? She didn't have the nerve to follow him.

This was one conversation she was relieved to let drop.

T.J. SLEPT ON THE COUCH that night. In the morning he was gone by the time she came into the kitchen to try and force herself to eat some breakfast.

She made it through the day at work, thanks to the kids in her class. Their energy always drew her in, and often left her exhausted by the end of the day.

Today, all she wanted was to drag her body home and collapse on the sofa with a good book. But Karen came by to talk to her. Heather could tell she had something important to say.

"I went to the doctor last week."

"And?"

She dropped her gaze to the floor. "I'm pregnant."

"Well." It was hard to know what to say. Congratulations were hardly in order. "I guess you weren't surprised."

"No. But I was pretty upset. Then I made the mistake of telling Ryan this weekend."

"He didn't take it well?"

"Not well at all." Karen buried half her face with one hand. "He was really, really angry."

"Not at you, surely?"

"He acted like this was something I had *planned.* As if! I wish he could know what it feels like to be in this situation—like your body is some kind of traitor. I don't want to be pregnant. I wish it would all just go away."

Heather wondered if she was serious, or just venting. "Well, you do have that choice, Karen."

"I know. And that's exactly what Ryan wants me to do."

Heather wasn't surprised.

"He says we're too young to be parents. He doesn't plan on letting anything get in the way of his plans for law school."

Heather wondered if Karen had nursed a secret desire that Ryan would ask her to marry him. Probably she had. How disillusioned she must be feeling right now.

"Well, Ryan has a point," she argued on his behalf. "Neither of you are in the best position to be parents right now. And eighteen *is* very young to be married."

"I know, I know." Karen sounded so weary. And so old, all of a sudden. "But his solution is terribly easy from his point of view. He just has to drive me to a clinic, pay some money and presto! The problem is gone."

"Yes."

"Not so easy for me. I'm the one that has to have the operation and take the risk of any complications.

And I'm the one who'll feel guilty about this for the rest of my life!''

Heather wished she could offer words that would make this easier. She took Karen's hands in hers. ''You have to make a decision that *you* can live with. Ryan is the father, and you're right to consult him. But, as you know all too well, this is happening to *your* body. Not to his.''

Karen blinked away a sheen of tears. ''I just wish he could see this from my perspective. But he doesn't even try.''

''What about your parents?''

''I haven't told them. How can I? They probably think I'm still a virgin. What a nightmare…''

''You'll get through this, Karen.'' Heather went to give her former student a hug. If only Karen knew just how completely she empathized with her situation. But Karen didn't know the story of Heather's first pregnancy. Secrets could be kept in a small town only if you were very, very careful.

But right now, Karen needed to know that she wasn't alone. That other women, all sorts of women, had gone through the same thing.

''Karen, can I tell you something in complete confidence?''

Karen nodded solemnly and Heather told her about her first pregnancy. ''I dropped out of university that fall and had to repeat the year after the baby was born.''

She didn't tell Heather who the father had been, or admit how painful it had been to give up her baby. She just wanted Karen to know she wasn't alone.

"I can't believe it, Ms. Collins. I never would have guessed."

"The main thing is that getting pregnant didn't ruin my life. That's what I want you to focus on, Karen. You will get through this, no matter how difficult it may seem right now."

HER MIND WAS FOCUSED on Karen's problems when Heather ran into Russ in the staff room, photocopying an assignment for the next day.

Remembering T.J.'s bitter accusation of the previous night, she felt her face color with embarrassment. Quickly she turned to the sink and made a thorough job of washing her mug.

"How was your day?" Russ asked.

She thought about the fight with T.J., Karen's upsetting news and now her new self-consciousness. "I've had better."

Russ patted her shoulder sympathetically on his way to the door. "The Boychuk twins?"

"Not this time."

He paused, waiting. Heather still couldn't look at him. They'd been friends for so long, they could always tell when something was wrong with the other person. But this was one problem she couldn't share with Russ. *My husband thinks I'm still in love with you.*

No, she didn't dare say that.

THAT NIGHT HEATHER HAD THE dream again. She awoke with her pajamas sweaty, her heart racing. She disentangled herself from the covers, leaving T.J. sleeping peacefully.

At least he was in bed with her again. Even if they'd barely spoken to each other all evening.

After putting on her slippers and robe she wandered to the kitchen where she warmed some milk, then prowled restlessly.

It seemed that every night after Karen came to talk to her, this was happening. She wished she knew how to make the dream go away. She didn't want to be crippled by the decision she'd made fifteen years ago. She needed to move on. For the sake of this new baby. And for herself and T.J....

Heather paced the kitchen, the living room, eventually making her way to the office. They were planning to move all this furniture downstairs to make room for the baby. They'd have to do it soon. She wondered if T.J. felt overwhelmed, too, at how quickly this all seemed to be happening.

With her first pregnancy, the nine months had dragged. They'd been almost pure torture. But this time, she wished she could slow time down. Since this might be her last child, she wanted to enjoy every stage to its fullest. Even the hugely pregnant and uncomfortable last trimester.

Heather brushed a hand over the filing cabinets, wondering how on earth T.J. was going to carry these downstairs. As she did so, her hand hit against an envelope.

It was the report T.J. had commissioned. Tentatively, she pulled it down and read the label, then the return address. *Maurice Waters, Private Investigator...*

She sank to the floor and sat cross-legged, with the envelope in her lap.

Was T.J. right? Had her feelings for Russ and her feelings for the baby she'd given away somehow become mixed into one package? By clinging to one, was she also hanging on to the other?

Even if that were true, would anything in this report help?

Heather held the envelope up to the light. She couldn't read through the thick colored paper. After another brief pause, she unfolded the metal clasp that held the envelope closed. Just as she was about to pull out the report, she heard a sound in the hall.

Footsteps.

T.J. appeared at the office door. His gaze dropped from her face to the envelope in her hand. Without saying a word he watched as she pulled out the report.

She scanned the typed pages that told a story of a

well-adjusted boy who earned good grades at school
and loved basketball. Photographs showed a doting
mother and father, and a happy, adolescent boy who
looked so much like Russ it made her heart ache. A
chocolate brown lab was in every picture, always
close to the boy.

Jason. They'd named him Jason.

"Nice family, huh?" T.J. had moved into the
room and was looking at the pictures over her shoulder.

"Couldn't be better." She compressed her lips,
fighting tears. Seeing all this now, she wondered why
she'd resisted the truth for so long. It was wonder-
fully reassuring to see for herself that she'd made the
right decision.

"It's too bad about the hair, though."

"What are you talking about?"

"Jason. The kid. He inherited your red hair."

Heather had been on the verge of tears. Now she
had to laugh. "You are impossible. Will you never
grow up?"

"Probably not. But come to bed, anyway. Mrs.
Manley will see the lights and think we're up arguing."

As Heather's gaze fell to the photo in her lap, his
voice grew more gentle. "You can look at those
again, tomorrow. Come on, Heather. It's late."

Reluctantly she let him pull her from the cold

floor. Immediately she realized he was right. She was exhausted.

"Sleep tight," he told her, tucking her under the covers.

She dropped off before he made it to the other side of the bed. And this time, no nightmares of any sort disturbed her slumber.

THE NEXT DAY AFTER SCHOOL, T.J. called to say he'd be late.

"Sorry, Heather. I'd planned to get home early to make dinner, but the staff decided it was time to decorate for Christmas, and we've got a huge mess here. I need to get this sorted out before we open for business tomorrow."

"That's fine. Don't worry. And thanks for calling." Heather hung up the phone with a feeling of wonderment. This was the first time, *ever,* he'd called to say he would be late. Surely a good sign.

She made herself a simple meal, then read while she ate it.

Time slipped away. Soon it was almost eight. With a sigh—just how long did it take to put up a Christmas tree and a few strands of fairy lights?—she put aside her book and tidied the kitchen.

She was about to turn on the television, when she finally heard footsteps on the front landing. The door wasn't locked—she'd left it open for T.J. She was surprised at how glad she felt to have him finally home. She dropped the remote control and wondered if this might be the time T.J. gave her a kiss when he walked in the door.

But T.J. didn't walk inside her house. Ryan Farrell did. The eighteen-year-old stood on her welcome mat, his eyes cold and hard.

"Ryan? What are you doing?"

"I need to talk to you." He had on jeans, a ski jacket, and an angry expression.

"Ryan, this is my home, not the school. You need permission to come inside."

"Your door wasn't locked."

As if that was the point. She told herself not to be alarmed by his odd behavior. Ryan was a former student, a good kid, if a trifle too intense. He wasn't going to do anything stupid.

But hadn't he already done something stupid? He'd gotten his girlfriend pregnant. Sweet, smart Karen Boychuk, who thought the world revolved around this guy.

"Ryan, what's going on here?" She moved a bit closer, almost blanching when she recognized the smell of alcohol coming off the school aged kid.

"I need to talk to you."

"Not tonight. It's late, and you've been drinking. Why don't we make an appointment and you can meet me in the classroom."

"I want to talk *now*."

"I'm sure you do, but right now isn't convenient

for me. I'm expecting T.J. home any second. Please leave, Ryan.'' When he didn't budge, she added, more firmly, ''This is my house. And I'm telling you to get out.''

At that, Ryan smiled. It wasn't a pleasant smile. His eyes remained hard and focused. On her.

''Your husband is still at the hardware store. The lights were on and I could see right in the window. Judging from the mess in there, he's going to be a while.''

Oh, damn. Heather glanced at the portable phone on a table nearby. Should she dash for it? Or would that just get Ryan riled? If this came down to a physical match between the two of them she had no doubt who would win. Ryan was a full-grown man now.

Maybe she'd be wise to let him say his piece, blow off a little steam, and *then* get him out of here. ''Okay, Ryan.'' She settled her fists at her hips. ''You want to talk? Then do it.''

''I came here to tell you to leave Karen alone.'' He pointed a finger at her. ''I know she told you about…about the situation. But it's really none of your business. So don't go telling her what to do.''

Of course, she'd known his visit had to have something to do with the baby. ''I've never told Karen what to do. I don't even invite her to my classroom. She comes on her own, because she wants to.''

If you were any kind of a boyfriend, she'd be leaning on you right now. She wouldn't need me at all,

Heather felt like adding. But she tempered her message a little. "Karen is scared and she feels alone. She needs a lot of support right now."

Ryan slammed a hand on the wall. "She wouldn't have to be scared if she'd just take care of the situation."

"Are you talking about an abortion?"

"Damn right that's what I'm talking about."

"That's a big step. Karen has to make sure it's the right decision for her."

"What about me? I'm the father. Don't I get any say in this?"

"You may be the father. But the pregnancy is happening to *Karen's* body. Not yours."

"So what are you saying? You want her to have this baby?"

Slowly Ryan had been working his way into the house. The snow he was tracking onto her carpet was Heather's last concern. *Damn it, T.J. Come home!*

"I'm well aware that my opinion doesn't count in this situation. I just don't like to see Karen pressured to do something she isn't comfortable with."

Ryan took another step toward her. Raising his hand, he jabbed his finger in her direction. "Karen *had* her mind made up until you started messing with it. She loves me and she would do exactly what I told her if it wasn't for you."

Heather hoped that wasn't true. Yes, Karen was

crazy about Ryan. But surely she was too smart to be manipulated.

"I have plans for my life. I'm leaving this town and going to law school. It's what I've wanted all my life and I'm not giving up my dreams because of some stupid mistake."

The young man's face reflected pure determination. "I'm going to make something of myself. And not you, or Karen, are going to stop me."

"Ryan, believe me I understand how you feel. I just wish you would calm down so that we could talk about the situation rationally. In fact, why don't I call Karen and we—"

"No! I don't want you to talk to Karen. Haven't you understood anything I've said?" He took several more steps, forcing her backward, pushing her right up to the edge of the sofa. He leaned in a few inches, bringing his face, and his foul breath, into an uncomfortable range.

"You're not my teacher anymore. And I'm not a kid. Leave my girlfriend alone? You understand?"

Heather was sure he was going to hit her. He had such a crazy light in his eye, and his mouth twisted in a mean, vicious way. But just then the front door opened again. T.J. burst inside.

"What the hell is going on here?"

Ryan backed right off. "We were just talking, Mr. Collins."

"Didn't look like talking to me." T.J. lost no time

striding across the room, grasping for the collar of the boy's jacket. Ryan was the same height, but he didn't have near T.J.'s muscle mass. The boy's bravado visibly dissipated.

"I didn't mean any harm."

"I don't believe that for a minute, Ryan." Finally Heather found her voice. "You came into this house, uninvited, and dared to threaten me."

"Is that right?" T.J. pulled up on the collar until the boy was forced to lift his head at an odd angle. "You leave my wife alone, kid. Get it? Heather, call the RCMP."

She picked up the phone she'd gazed at so longingly before. Quickly she dialed the number as T.J. focused again on Ryan.

"We'll see what the police have to say about your story, kid. There are laws in this town, you know. You can't just—"

But Ryan wasn't having any of that. With one violent lunge, he broke free of T.J.'s grip and bolted for the door.

"Damn!" T.J. was a half second behind him.

Ryan slipped out the front door, T.J. on his heels.

"Stop, T.J." Heather stood in her slippered feet on the cold landing, phone in hand, watching her husband give chase to the young man. Despite T.J.'s speed, Ryan managed to disappear behind Mrs. Manley's tall hedge of junipers.

T.J. gave up the chase. In the cold, still night they

heard an ignition grind. The sound of tires gripping, crunching against snow.

"Let him go, T.J.," Heather called out. "The police will track him down. It's not like they don't know where he lives. I just hope he doesn't hurt anyone, driving impaired like that."

T.J. nodded, then turned and slowly made his way back to the house. Once he was inside, Heather shut and bolted the door.

"My fault for leaving that unlocked," she said.

"Not your fault at all. That kid is crazy. What was he doing here?"

As Heather struggled for an answer, he suddenly realized she was trembling. "Come here." He opened his arms and pulled her close. "It's okay, sweetheart. I'm not going to let him near you again."

## CHAPTER SIXTEEN

HEATHER AND T.J. REPORTED Ryan's actions to the police. Heather decided she didn't want to press charges. "Just go talk to him," she told the officer who came to the house to take their statements.

"Give him a good scare," T.J. advised.

"Don't be too hard on him—he's just a kid." The more time that lapsed, the more Heather convinced herself she'd mistaken Ryan's intentions. She was positive he hadn't meant to hurt her. Or even scare her, necessarily. He was just terribly distressed. And confused.

After the RCMP officer left, Heather finally explained the whole situation to T.J.

"Ryan's upset because his girlfriend is pregnant. I'd been talking to her, and he felt I was unfairly advising her against an abortion, which is what he wants her to have."

"I've seen those kids together. Karen Boychuk, right? I know her dad. He's either the worst farmer in the area, or the most unlucky. He's always coming into town to get a part for something that's broken down."

"His wife works at the nursing home. She's been on the school council several times. She takes a fairly conservative—almost strict—stand on most issues."

"You think they'll be hard on Karen when she tells them she's pregnant?" T.J. handed Heather a mug of sweet tea. He'd made himself a quick sandwich after the officer left, and now they were both on the sofa, facing each other.

"I don't know. Probably," honesty compelled her to admit, "but hopefully they'll come around."

"Yeah, she'll need their support, given that loser boyfriend she has."

"You know, I actually feel some sympathy for Ryan."

"Are you kidding me?"

"One thing he said to me tonight is true. He has a great future ahead of him. He's bright, good-looking, willing to apply himself. I don't blame him for feeling derailed by all that has happened."

T.J. leaned over to touch a lock of her hair. In his eyes she saw a hint of the gentleness she usually only glimpsed in bed.

"I guess you can relate, huh?"

She nodded, overcome with sadness. Helplessness.

"One mistake and it changes your life forever."

T.J. shifted even closer. Cupped his hand to her head. "Don't think back, Heather. Think forward."

She smiled, just as a tear slipped out of her eye. With the side of his thumb, T.J. erased the dampness.

"You were right about that report, T.J. Reading about Jason's life, well, it really did help. Even seeing the pictures wasn't as painful as I'd expected."

She'd been so sure that if she found out even a little about the baby she'd had so long ago, she'd have the overwhelming urge to go out and claim him as her own. Instead she felt simply peace and acceptance.

Because of her decision to carry him to term, this wonderful, healthy boy was alive in the world. His parents had never managed to adopt or give birth to any other children, and it was obvious from the photos the investigator had taken that Jason was their world.

T.J. swallowed. She could tell he was still nervous. "Did it make you want to see him? Add to your regret?"

"Not at all. It's the strangest thing. I didn't feel at all the way I expected to feel. Made me wish I'd done this much sooner."

"What if he tries to find you one day?"

"I'd welcome that, T.J. But even if he does decide to meet me, I know he'll never think of me as his mother. He already has a mom, and a dad, too, and an entire extended family. I'm just...I don't know...really *glad* for him."

"Heather?"

"What?"

"You never cease to amaze me."

"Likewise." She put her hand over his. "Thank you, T.J. Thank you for finding him for me."

THE NEXT DAY, HEATHER WAITED around after school in case Karen dropped in for a visit. She didn't. Heather wished she had some way of knowing if this was Karen's choice, or if Ryan had intimidated her.

She was wondering if she ought to check up on the young woman, when she almost bumped into Russ. They'd left their respective classrooms at the same time and met at the center of the hall.

"Excuse me," she apologized. "I wasn't watching where I was going."

He shifted his briefcase to his other hand, so he could pick up her bag, which had fallen to the floor. An envelope had slid out and he stuffed it back in without checking the label. Heather glanced in either direction. The school was deserted. At least on this level.

"Russ, I need to talk to you about something."

"Sure. Is it private?"

She didn't know how he knew, he just did. She nodded.

"Let's go into my classroom, then."

Once they were inside, he closed the door and faced her. Behind the curiosity in his eyes, she saw just a hint of apprehension. Was she wrong to bring this up to him now? She knew he was happy with his family and preoccupied with finishing the new house for Christmas.

But maybe he had nights, like her, when he woke up from a bad dream and just wondered. She felt she owed him the choice, at least.

"Russ, a while ago T.J. hired a private investigator. He asked him to find the baby that I'd given up for adoption." *Our baby,* she amended silently.

Russ's complexion went pale, his expression solemn.

"It's a long story, but it boils down to this. The investigator found him and he took some photographs and wrote a short report about his home and his family, friends and school life."

Russ's gaze dropped to her briefcase.

"Yes, it was in that envelope."

"Oh, hell, Heather." Russ looked up at the ceiling and raked the fingers of his free hand through his hair. He exhaled a loud breath, then said again, "Hell!"

"Maybe I shouldn't have said anything." She made for the door, but Russ put out a hand to stop her.

"No. Sorry if I seem kind of stressed. I'm glad you told me."

But he was just being polite. Heather could tell that he *wasn't* glad she'd told him. Not at all. "Forget it, Russ. Okay? You don't need to look at the report. I just thought I should let you know that I have it. If you ever want—'' She broke off. Swallowed. Shook her head.

"I should be going." She headed for the door again, but Russ was in the way and he didn't step aside for her. Instead, he put a hand on her shoulder.

"It's just that Julie and I only recently came to terms with the whole idea of me having another child."

"I understand."

"I don't want to upset her. Not when everything's going so well."

"I said I *understand*."

Russell frowned, but he didn't try to stop her this time when she made another move for the door. Nor did he follow her as she headed down the old wood staircase to collect her coat and boots from the staff room.

T.J. MADE A STIR-FRY FOR dinner that evening. Heather was finding she needed to stick to lighter food now, and smaller portions. There just wasn't room in her stomach for very much. Nor in her bladder, either.

"No trouble with Ryan Farrell today, I hope?" T.J. dished up their supper and poured her a glass of milk.

"I haven't seen him since last night."

"Good."

Heather paused over her meal, contemplating her

husband. She'd been so happy to find him home this afternoon, ahead of her for a change. In fact, the buzz of excitement, the thrill of having him reach out to kiss her, had her speculating about her feelings for him.

She'd always been hypersensitive to T.J.'s presence, whether in the classroom when they were kids, or in their house now that they were married. She wondered if she'd disliked him quite as much as she'd thought. Maybe her feelings had been more complicated than she'd ever admitted.

"T.J., what really happened between you and Lynn?"

His fork froze in midair. He set the food back on his plate and regarded her with a distinct lack of pleasure. "Heather, I told you all about my first marriage long ago."

"Only that you put in too many hours at work." He'd definitely painted himself as the bad guy. "But how did Lynn come to marry someone else so quickly?"

T.J.'s eyes narrowed. "What do you mean?"

"You came back to Chatsworth after she moved to Toronto with this other guy. Which was just after the divorce, right? So she must have been seeing him when you were still married. Did their relationship start after you were separated?"

"Do we have to discuss this?" T.J. got up and scraped the remains of his dinner into the garbage.

"I think we do." She followed him, not wanting him to put too much distance between them. She touched his arm. "Your wife had an affair, didn't she? While you were at work, trying to provide for your family, she was starting something new with this other guy."

T.J.'s muscles tensed under her touch. She could tell he hadn't thought of the situation that way before.

"It was my fault Lynn was so lonely. I neglected her. Left all the work of raising our child in her hands."

There he went, trying to skewer himself with guilt again. Why? Why was T.J. so anxious to shoulder the blame for his marriage break-up?

"Who was the guy, T.J.? How did she meet him?"

At first she thought she'd been too intrusive, that T.J. was going to retreat and withdraw, his usual pattern. But to her surprise, he started to talk.

"Jeff Philips was one of my colleagues at work. He started with the firm the same year I did, the same year as Lynn, too."

"Lynn's a lawyer?" Heather hadn't realized that.

"Yes. The three of us quickly made friends, and almost as quickly Lynn and I became a couple. We married a year after we passed the bar. After she had Sally, Lynn took extended maternity leave, then decided she wanted to be a full-time mother. I supported that decision, because it made it easier for me to put in the kind of hours I needed to make partner.''

"But Lynn didn't sacrifice her career for yours. She *wanted* to stay home with Sally?"

T.J. blinked a few times. "Yeah. I guess that's right.''

"And when did she and Jeff start their affair?"

"I don't really know. Maybe it was the time I couldn't make it to our sixth anniversary celebration. I told her to take someone else to the play. We already had the tickets and a baby-sitter booked.'' T.J. frowned. "She never did tell me who she went with.''

"Oh, T.J. How much longer after that did your marriage end?"

She waited as he went through the mental calculations.

"I guess about four months. Lynn said she was tired of raising our child on her own. She said she saw more of my best friend than she did of me.''

"Your best friend being Jeff."

He nodded.

"Some best friend.'' Heather wasn't sure how Lynn had managed to make him feel like he was in the wrong in this situation. "Dammit, T.J. Maybe you shouldn't have spent so much time at work. But they deceived you. Didn't you feel angry?"

"Did I have the right? If I wasn't willing to be a

husband and father, how could I blame Lynn for looking elsewhere?''

''Elsewhere being your best friend? And while she was still living in your house, sleeping in your bed? T.J., you weren't the only guilty party. Not by far.''

T.J. WENT OUT FOR A RUN. He needed to clear his head. Think through the implications of his talk with Heather.

The winter solstice was only a couple of weeks away. It had been dark for hours. The temperature, already well below freezing, was still dropping. But with his layered jackets, running mask and gloves, T.J. felt warm enough. He started at a fast pace toward Willow Road, intending to run to the lake and back. The common route was one he knew Julie Matthew covered regularly.

He didn't see her out tonight, though. Probably too cold. He didn't see anyone, not even the headlights of a passing vehicle. There was a cross-country ski trail that drew visitors to the lake during the daytime, but on winter evenings, this road was pretty deserted.

The solitude was just what he needed. For a while he concentrated on the sound of his shoes crunching into the hard snow pack on the road. The huff, huff, huff of his breath in the dead winter calm.

Slowly, slowly, a sense of righteous anger began to grow. Oddly it was Jeff he felt the most betrayed by, not Lynn.

He and Jeff had worked together on so many projects. Right up until the end, they'd gone out on their regular lunches where they'd trusted each other with everything, consulting about cases and office politics, confiding their own personal ambitions with utter candor.

Everything except Jeff's growing feelings for Lynn and…the embezzlement.…

T.J. had begun to realize something strange was going on with a few of the firm's trust accounts. Not wanting to make accusations before he had the facts, he began to work even longer hours, gathering information that pointed to an old-timer with heart problems—Vince Macarthur—as the culprit. Finally, he'd put together enough evidence to nail Macarthur. But the day before he was scheduled to meet with the executive committee of the law firm to disclose his findings, Lynn had told him she was in love with Jeff. She wanted a divorce.

He'd missed the appointment, forgotten all about it. He'd forgotten other appointments, too, screwed up on several important accounts.

Always the solicitous friend, Jeff had helped cover his client obligations for him. At the time T.J. had been grateful. What a solid guy, he'd thought, never quite making the connection that for months, Jeff had been secretly meeting with Lynn. Sleeping with T.J.'s wife.

Dammit to hell, why had he ever considered that man his friend?

# CHAPTER SEVENTEEN

T.J. WAS QUIET WHEN HE returned from his run, but Heather figured that was a good thing. Much as she wanted to talk to him and help him deal with the quagmire of emotions he had to be feeling, she realized he needed to sort his thoughts out on his own first. She only hoped that as he reviewed the circumstances leading up to his divorce, he'd remember the blame wasn't all his.

Interesting how quick he'd been to accept that load. Heather couldn't help but wonder if his father was to blame. Old Theodore Collins was a hard-nosed man. T.J. had been forced to work part-time at the store all throughout high school. She'd seen Theodore rail on his son when things went wrong. T.J. had been pretty lippy in return, but deep down, his father's criticisms must have made their mark.

Heather found herself distracted in the classroom the next day. Several times Perry and Paul got the best of her with their silly antics. She refrained from asking them about their sister. If Karen wanted to talk to her, she knew where to find her.

But Heather suspected she'd seen the last of

Karen's visits. Ryan Farrell's will had obviously pre-
vailed. Which made Heather wonder if perhaps she'd
underestimated the potential threat that boy was to
Karen's well-being. As the father of her unborn baby,
he definitely had a stake in the situation. But he had
no right to browbeat Karen. Or to tell her whom she
could and could not talk to.

More and more troubled by the situation, Heather
reversed her decision to stay out of it. She had to
make sure Karen was okay. After class she asked
Perry for directions to the farm, then drove out on
the country roads to the ranch house where the family of five lived.

She found Karen in the kitchen peeling potatoes
for supper. The boys were out playing in the snow,
while their father milked cows. Mrs. Boychuk
wouldn't be home from the nursing home for another
two hours.

"Karen, I'm sorry if me being here is uncomfortable for you. It's just that I haven't seen you in a
while. I wanted to make sure that was your choice.
That Ryan hasn't warned you to stay away from me
or anything." She laughed, as if to suggest such a
thing was ridiculous.

But Karen's grim expression showed no reciprocal
amusement. In her tight jeans and short T-shirt,
her young body showed no trace of her pregnancy.
Heather remembered that she'd been able to keep her
own condition secret up to her fifth month thanks

to a judicious choice of clothing. And Karen wasn't yet three months.

The perfect time to terminate the pregnancy. If, indeed, that was what Karen wanted.

"Ryan *did* tell me not to talk to you anymore," Karen finally admitted. "He said this baby was our business and that I had no right to discuss our plans with anyone but him."

"Is that the way you feel, too?" Heather asked gently. She was moved by the condition of the room. Everything was old, but very clean. Since Karen's mother worked full-time, Karen probably was responsible for the immaculate housekeeping.

That must be a lot of work, especially when she had to watch her brothers and cook, as well. No wonder Karen was so anxious to move on and move up. But did she really see marriage to Ryan as her only ticket out of Chatsworth?

"I like talking to you," Karen confessed in a rush. "I've missed our after-school visits. But Ryan's so sure an abortion is the right thing to do. We went for a preliminary consultation yesterday. And booked an appointment for the—operation."

"I see. And you're okay with this?"

"Not really." Karen's voice shook. "Last night I tried to tell him I couldn't go through with it."

"And what was Ryan's reaction?"

"Oh, he was so angry. I've never seen him like that before."

"Sometimes you don't really know a person until you see how they react under pressure."

Karen was quick to defend her boyfriend. "When the time is right, he'll make a great father. He's just so young is all. We're both too young."

"I know." Heather could certainly commiserate on that point.

"He swore he would break up with me if I didn't have this abortion. He says if I have the baby, he won't have anything to do with it. Oh, Ms. Collins, I don't know what to do!"

"That may be how he feels now. But he may change his mind in time. Besides, like it or not, Ryan has a legal obligation to your child."

"I don't want to *force* Ryan to pay me money. He'll never learn to love the baby that way. Besides, if I kept this baby, I wouldn't just want money from Ryan. I'd want our child to have a *father.*"

Yes. Oh, yes. Heather could so relate to the way Karen felt. She knew that many children were raised successfully by single mothers. But for her and Russ's baby, that hadn't seemed right to her.

"Every pregnant woman has to decide for themselves based on the options open to them at the time. Just so you know, abortion isn't your only choice. Nor is raising this child on your own, if Ryan truly does break up with you."

Karen's chin dropped. She used the back of her

hand to swipe at her eyes. "You're talking about the decision you made—adoption."

"I'm not saying it's right for you. Only that it's an option. Karen, you've been carrying this load on your own for too long. You need to talk to your parents."

Karen shook her head. "You don't know my mother. She has ideas about the way things should be. She's more excited about me going to university than I am."

"I know how hard it feels to disappoint your parents. But they may surprise you. Mine did."

"I'm just so scared."

Heather wanted to put her arm around the young woman. But Karen had been maintaining a careful distance between them. Heather suspected she wasn't totally comfortable with her being there.

"Putting it off won't make it easier."

"Unless I have the abortion," Karen whispered.

She returned to her task of peeling potatoes. Heather suspected she was crying, but couldn't tell for sure. Again, the urge to comfort was strong. But again, she felt a countering reluctance to invade Karen's privacy.

"I should probably go. If you ever want to find me, to talk things over, you know where to look."

It was more difficult to leave than Heather expected. Her heart ached for the young woman. She'd suffered so much, already. And the hardest part was yet to come.

T.J. WASN'T HOME BY THE TIME Heather returned from the Boychuks' farm. Needing to talk, Heather decided to drive over to the hardware store and find him. She passed by the post office, the bank, the new sweet shop and came to a stop outside the front window of the Handy Hardware.

The Christmas display dazzled in the large picture window, a homey scene of a traditional Christmas including a tree, fake fireplace, stockings and presents. Beyond the window, the store was dark, obviously closed. But a faint light glowed from the back.

Perhaps T.J. was working in the storage area.

Heather maneuvered out of her car—with her bulk no longer a simple task—then pocketed the keys. The front doors were locked, so she tried knocking. Eventually T.J. released the catch and swung open the heavy wooden door.

"Heather? It isn't time, is it?"

She traced the outline of her tummy through the heavy wool coat. "Don't panic. No, everything's fine."

His eyes narrowed. He gave her a look she remembered from their school years, a look she'd never managed to decipher.

"What are you doing here?"

"Just wondered when you'd be home for dinner."

"Why didn't you phone?"

"I'm not sure," she admitted. "But I might have if I'd known you were going to make me wait out here in the cold."

He stepped aside then, making room for her to come in and then closing the door after her. "You never drop by the store, you know."

His comment was true. "That's thanks to your conditioning. Do you remember what a hard time you used to give me when my parents sent me here on an errand? I used to dread running into you."

The devilish grin he gave her showed no sign of remorse. "But what about later, Heather? When I moved back to Chatsworth I figured I'd see you in here now and then. Never did."

Again, he was right. She *had* avoided him. And for good reason. Being with T.J. had always spelled danger…of one sort or another.

Now she saw him looking at her in a way that ought to be impossible. She was almost full-term in her pregnancy. He couldn't want her now. Here.

Impossible.

And yet, she knew that look.

He reached out to touch a strand of her hair, a seductive glint in his eyes. "I wonder if you're here because you need a little…attention from your husband?"

That had been the last thought on her mind. But suddenly her heart was racing, her face felt flushed.

Heather finally had to admit that this unacknowledged attraction between them had been at the root of her discomfort with this man for a very long time, probably dating all the way back to high school.

What would he say if she confessed that to him now? She knew she didn't dare. Knowledge was power, and T.J. already had more than his fair share.

"Don't flatter yourself, T.J." She moved beyond the reach of his arm, pretending to inspect a display of appliances. "So what's keeping you so late?"

T.J. shrugged. "Nothing important. I was just rearranging some of the inventory items in the back."

"Yeah?"

"And thinking," he admitted. "After closing hours the store is nice and quiet. It's a good time to mull things over."

"Do you still miss her, T.J.?" Heather hoped she hadn't read his mood wrong, but she suspected her recalcitrant husband might actually be in the mood to talk.

"Sally?"

Was he being deliberately obtuse? *"Lynn."*

His half smile told her he'd known whom she'd meant from the beginning. "No, I don't miss Lynn. In the beginning I regretted losing her friendship. I still regret that. But I don't think I ever really loved her."

"You must have. You married her."

"There's an intimacy that's fostered when you

work closely with someone, the way she and I did in our articling days. I felt connected to her then, but unfortunately after our marriage we were assigned to different departments in the firm. Those feelings eventually faded, but they weren't replaced with anything else.''

"So you don't resent your friend for stealing her away?''

T.J. shifted his gaze to the right, then down to the floor. His chest heaved with a heavy sigh. "That's a tough one. I think I resent that he has Sally, more than anything. So what if I made partner a year before he did? He had his priorities figured out. He's such a damn good father. Why couldn't I have been that kind of dad?''

"You made mistakes. It doesn't matter why.'' Surely he'd been influenced by his own father who had practically lived for his store, rather than his family.

"You can be whatever kind of dad you want to be, T.J. Sally's only four. And our baby isn't even born yet.''

T.J. took a step toward her. "You always see the sunny side, don't you, Heather Beatrice Sweeney?''

"I try,'' she admitted, stepping backward as he moved toward her again. She slipped behind the display she'd been admiring earlier. He came round from the right side.

She felt like they were playing a slow-motion game of tag. He was "it" and she was his prey.

"Just tell me one thing," she bargained, as she moved past blenders into toasters.

"One thing," he agreed. He was on her trail, graduating from mix masters to coffeemakers.

"Do you know that there's some talk in town that you embezzled money from your law firm?"

He stopped smack in the middle of electric frying pans. For a moment he just seemed confounded. Then he laughed. "Figures. The small-town rumor mill. Never underestimate it."

"But how did the rumor get started?

"I can guess. One of the Hoggart boys is a lawyer in Calgary. The business community is tight. He must have heard the story and passed it on to his parents."

"But what story could he have heard?"

"What's the matter, Heather? Afraid you've married a crook?"

"No," she said without hesitation. "I know you would never do anything like that. I'm just puzzled about the rumors."

"Well, there *was* a problem at the firm where I used to work. I had accumulated some information proving who the guilty party was—one of the original partners, Vince Macarthur. Then Lynn dropped her bombshell and I forgot all about it. About a month after I'd started work at the hardware I received a call from one of my former law partners. They'd discovered the missing money on their own.''

''Did they press charges against Vince Macarthur?''

''Actually, no. Vince managed to convince them that *I* was the one who'd taken the money.''

''But that's awful!''

''Not really. They didn't have any proof. They weren't able to go to the police.''

''But what about your reputation?''

He shrugged. ''At that point in my life, I didn't care about that.''

''You astound me, T.J. You really do.'' How could he be so detached? ''There has to be something you can do to clear your name.''

''Of course there is. All I have to do is take that file of information to the executive committee as I originally planned.''

''You still have it?''

''Sure.'' He moved past pans and into the blenders. He was almost at toasters.

''Well, thank goodness. I think you'd better do something about this, T.J.''

But her husband seemed to have forgotten about the embezzlement situation. He was continuing to advance on her. Now he was within touching distance. She wondered if he noticed she wasn't moving away anymore.

"You want me to go to Calgary?" He put a hand to her head, pulled her in close. Very close.

"Not really." She couldn't breathe all of a sudden. She didn't want him anywhere but *here*. With her.

T.J. was moving in for a kiss. His eyes were half closed. She stepped on tiptoe to meet him, wrapping her arms around his neck. After a warm, thorough melding of lips, mouths, tongues, she pulled back a fraction of an inch.

"But maybe you should."

He eased his grip on her slightly so he could get a better look at her face. "What does it matter? I don't care what those old farts think."

"Maybe not now. But one day you may. Your *children* may care. And I think setting the story straight would help you put what happened in Calgary behind you. I'm talking about everything, T.J. Not just the business stuff, but the affair and the divorce, too."

"If I tell you I'll think about it, will you have sex with me on the sofa in the coffee room?"

"T.J.!"

He grinned. "Or we could do it in bedding and towels, if you prefer. Just take about ten steps back…"

Oh, Lord. He wasn't taking any of this seriously. "I don't know what I'm going to do with you."

"That's okay. Because I've got quite a few ideas about what to do with you. And I think you'll like all of them.'' Then he whisked her into his arms and carried her to the very back of the dark, deserted store.

THEIR LOVEMAKING WAS SLOW and playful. Heather had never seen T.J. in such a lighthearted mood. At the end, though, when they were both satisfied and pleasantly exhausted, he turned somber.

''If I ask you something will you promise to tell me the truth?''

''I'll try.''

He buried his face in her neck. ''Do you ever think of Russ when we're making love? Have you ever?''

She pulled back so she could see his eyes. ''Never.''

''Truthfully?''

''Absolutely.''

''Not even the first time?''

Since he seemed to think this was important, Heather did her best to remember. It wasn't difficult. Every second she'd ever spent with T.J. seemed permanently etched in her memory. ''Maybe for the first couple of minutes. I remember thinking he'd be jealous if he knew what I was doing.''

Which had been the point of sleeping with T.J. in the first place. Only it hadn't taken long for her to find herself totally swept away in the moment.

T.J. seemed satisfied with her answers. She wondered if he would ask any other questions about Russ, but he didn't. He held her for another couple of minutes, then they both dressed and returned home.

## CHAPTER EIGHTEEN

AT SCHOOL THE NEXT WEEK, Russ sought out Heather during the beginning of lunch break. He caught her in her classroom as she erased that morning's lesson from the board.

"Heather? Mind if I talk to you a minute?"

He appeared edgy. Not a very usual state for Russ, who was normally difficult to unsettle.

"Sure."

He closed the door and approached her desk. "It's about that report you mentioned last week."

Heather put down the brush and devoted all her attention to him. "Yes?"

"I talked the situation over with Julie this weekend. She thinks we should take a look at it—if the offer's still open." He shoved his hands into his pockets, stared out the window to the field where Ben was probably running around in the snow right now.

"Are you sure?"

"I'd feel better knowing he was well taken care of. And happy." Russell turned from the view to look at her. "I hope that's the case."

"It is," she reassured him. "As it happens, I have the report with me. I thought you might have a change of heart. At first I was reluctant, too. I worried that the more I found out about Jason—"

"Jason?" Russ paused to consider the name. "That's good. I like it."

"Me, too." She smiled. "And he really looks like a Jason, too. Wait till you see the pictures." She dug the envelope out of her bag.

In two steps, Russell was beside her. He took the envelope eagerly from her hands, and in the process, his fingers brushed against hers.

"Thanks so much, Heather. Would it be all right if I took this home right now? I told Julie I might meet her for lunch. I'd kind of like the two of us to see this together."

"That's fine," Heather said, feeling a little dazed. She managed a small smile, but only until Russ was out of the classroom. Once she was alone, she collapsed into her chair, staring unseeingly across the room.

Gingerly she waited, expecting a feeling of hurt or at least mild resentment. Jason was *her* and Russ's child. Yet, he'd wanted to view the report with Julie.

But those feelings didn't come. She simply didn't care. If T.J. was right—if she *was* still in love with Russ—wouldn't she have felt *something?*

"I don't love Russell," she said to herself quietly. And for the first time in a long, long while, she really believed it.

THAT WEEKEND, HEATHER POINTED out to T.J. that there were only two more weeks until Christmas.

"Have you bought anything for Sally yet?"

He hadn't.

"If you hurry, we could still courier her something."

T.J. flipped the page of his newspaper. He was trying to ignore her, but it wasn't very easy. She'd woken up riled, and it seemed nothing he did would please her. Before breakfast she'd had him clearing out the second bedroom. She was determined to set up the baby crib and all the related paraphernalia today.

"I'm due in three weeks," she'd reminded him.

T.J. did not want to be reminded. He'd been avoiding the reality of this child ever since he'd married Heather. But time was indeed running out. Soon the baby would be here, a flesh-and-blood child that would need to be cared for—and loved.

It was his second chance at fatherhood and T.J. was scared to death. He didn't want to fail, didn't want to disappoint Heather. Yet, his track record didn't leave much room for hope.

"I'll need to run into Yorkton later this afternoon to pick up some basics—diapers, blankets, a couple of sleepers. Would you like me to buy Sally an outfit while I'm shopping? Maybe a pretty Christmas dress?" Heather buttered one of the muffins she'd baked that morning.

Where was her energy coming from all of a sudden?

"Does Sally like dresses, T.J.?"

"How the hell would I know?" He gave up on the paper, tossing it to the side. He guzzled the last of his lukewarm coffee, then headed for the hall closet.

"Where are you going?"

"To work. It'll be a busy day. It is two weeks before Christmas," he took perverse pleasure in reminding her.

She pushed herself out of her chair, then rested her hands on her hips, a posture that emphasized the enormous swelling of her abdomen. T.J. averted his eyes. Three more weeks. If Heather's doctor was right, that was all the time he had left before the baby came and changed everything. Lately, Heather had seemed warmer toward him. But when she saw for herself what a lousy father he was, that warmth would disappear.

"Do you think you could come home at lunchtime to put up the crib? I should have the wallpaper border finished by then."

*What's the rush?* he almost asked, then he glanced at the mound of her belly again, and stopped himself. "Yeah, I guess I could do that."

"Thanks."

T.J. was struck by how lovely his wife looked. Even at almost nine months pregnant. He thought she was particularly adorable in the denim overalls she wore today, with her long-sleeved pink top and her sassy red hair tied back from her face.

"Do you need me to bring home anything from the hardware?" He thought back to the list of items Lynn had taken him shopping for back when they'd been expecting Sally. "Do we need a diaper pail? A changing table?"

"I'm using Adrienne's old baby furniture. But a new diaper pail would be a good idea."

"Okay." He nodded, then shrugged on his coat and carried his boots to the front door. "Good, then. I'll see you at noon. Don't work too hard."

The wind hit him full in the face as he stepped out doors. It was a very frosty thirty below today. The sky was a frigid pale blue, the air almost hurt to breathe. They hadn't had any snow for a while, so the sidewalks were still clear. The forecast promised a storm later in the week, probably by Wednesday. So he'd be shoveling again before long.

It was ten minutes to nine when he arrived at Main Street. No time to stop at the café for a morning coffee. Since his marriage, he hadn't been doing that as much, anyway. But maybe he could squeeze in a quick stop at Lucky's.

He picked up a disposable camera there, exchanged a few words about the weather with Lucky at the till, then headed out again. He stopped in front of his store and took several pictures of the window display.

If he filled this roll today, he could drive into Yorkton tomorrow and drop it off at one of those one-hour places. He'd send some money, too. Tell Lynn to pick up something the kid would like.

T.J. headed to the cash register, tidying shelves on his way. In the toy aisle, he paused, recognizing one of the dolls from the pictures Sally had sent him. On the next shelf were some outfits, designed specifically to fit the dolls. Maybe he should send her a couple of these, as well as the photos and the money.

By the time T.J. had set aside a ski outfit and a glamorous dress that he hoped a little girl might like, he had his first customer of the day, followed soon by another.

Business flowed steadily all morning, and he almost forgot his promise to go home for lunch. One of his customers saved him when she wondered aloud what the noon special would be at the café that day.

"Lunch!" He glanced at his watch, then at Don who was at the register. "I need to go home and take care of something for Heather. Okay if I take an hour? You can have your break when I get back."

"No problem."

Carrying a large plastic container that ought to work fine as a diaper pail, T.J. walked briskly home. The enticing aroma of chicken soup greeted him when he opened the door. Heather puttered in the kitchen, a ladle in her hand.

She'd had a productive morning, he saw. A brightly colored wallpaper border of alphabet blocks encircled the baby's room. The carpet was freshly cleaned. New curtains hung over the window. He set the plastic pail unobtrusively in a corner.

"You've been busy," he said when he was in the kitchen again.

"Do you like it?"

"Yeah. It's nice."

He ate quickly, then took care of the crib for her. He moved the change table up from the basement, too, and the rocking chair that had also once belonged to Adrienne Jenson.

"Is that everything?" He dusted his hands together, although in actual fact there was no dust to remove. All the furniture had been spotlessly clean. Heather must have given it all a good scrubbing.

"I think so."

"Great. Well, I'll go back to the store then."

She came to the door to see him off. He paused, guessing from the expectant look on her face that she was waiting for a kiss, for him to say something loving and sweet. But he couldn't. Every day he loved her more and it killed him to know that she would never return his feelings. Not wholeheartedly.

Heather was sweet and kind to him because it was her nature. Not because she adored him the way he adored her.

SUNDAY MORNING, T.J. AWOKE before Heather. He lay watching her, marveling at the unpredictable events that had resulted in him getting the girl he'd always wanted for his wife.

They hadn't made love last night. He'd wanted to, but he could tell she was too exhausted. She'd spent all yesterday in a frenzy of activity, ignoring his advice to slow down a little.

As a result, they now had a fully stocked baby's room and Heather was completely worn out.

With effort, he resisted the urge to touch the fine skin on her cheek, or to twist one of her springy red curls. All his life he'd struggled with this desire to make physical contact with her. What was it about this particular woman?

He couldn't remember a time when she hadn't fascinated him. What would she say if she knew that he'd always been totally crazy about her?

Probably she'd feel sorry for him. Which was why he could never let her know how he really felt. He couldn't stand to be with a woman who pitied him. If he could have nothing else, at least he would have his pride and self-respect.

T.J. slipped out of the warm bed and headed for the bathroom. The time on the bedside clock read seven-fifteen. Outside, it was barely light. He tried to focus on the day's work ahead of him but something nagged at the back of his mind. He realized he couldn't put it off any longer.

Last week a strong, healthy-looking kid had stopped by wondering if T.J. had extra work. He was on break from university and could use a few bucks for the new term coming up. At the time, T.J. had offered him Thursday and Saturday. But maybe he could get Don to hire the kid for an extra few days...

He showered, shaved, brushed his teeth. The usual routine brought him no sense of comfort. In the kitchen, he set up the coffeemaker, then went down to the basement.

As well as his exercise equipment, he'd moved over from his apartment a metal, fireproof safe, about the size of a small microwave.

He worked the combination lock quickly open, then reached inside and pulled out the large envelope he'd placed in here several years ago.

Organized by date were statements from the bank, accounting ledgers of trust accounts, copies of letters from Vince Macarthur to his clients. Together these documents presented the clear and true story of what had been happening in the years before he'd left Macarthur, Edmond.

It was time someone else saw these documents. It was time he took his story public.

## CHAPTER NINETEEN

HEATHER DIDN'T WAKE UNTIL after ten. She couldn't believe she'd slept in so long, but she'd really worn herself out yesterday. T.J. had been right, she should have rested rather than gone shopping in Yorkton, but he'd never hear her admit it.

She ambled to the kitchen, expecting to find T.J. reading the weekend paper. But he wasn't there, nor was he in the basement lifting weights. She tightened the knot on her robe, best as she could, and returned to the kitchen.

Perhaps he'd left for Yorkton already. Hadn't he said he was going to develop those pictures for Sally today? She peered out the back window and saw that his truck was missing. Though a little disconcerted at finding herself alone, she was glad he'd decided to do something for his daughter for Christmas after all.

Christmas. She hadn't thought much about the holiday this year. Other than Sally's present, she and T.J. hadn't discussed the subject. Usually Heather decorated extravagantly for the holiday. But this year she hadn't yet pulled out the big plastic container where she kept her treasured ornaments and strands of colorful lights.

Her upcoming labor and the expectation of a new baby had overshadowed the holiday for her this season. Next year, when the baby would be almost one, she'd do the house up right. A real tree and outside lights and lots of home baking.

She was picturing it all in her head, when the phone rang. It turned out to be T.J.

"Where are you?" she asked. The line wasn't very clear.

"On my way to Calgary."

"What?"

"I'm going to settle that business we were talking about the other night."

Had her brain turned to mush? She'd heard that sometimes happened to pregnant women. Then, she finally realized what he was talking about.

"Do you have the file with you?"

"Yeah. I'm going to retain a lawyer and sort out this mess with Macarthur, Edmond."

Oh, she was so glad. T.J. should have done this years ago. And he would have, Heather felt certain, if his wife and best friend hadn't undermined his sense of self-worth.

She hated that Lynn had let him take the entire blame for the failure of their marriage. Even more, she'd made him feel he was an unreliable person.

"That's wonderful, T.J. But..."

"Is there a problem?"

"It's not really a problem. I think what you're doing is very, very important. But—it's only two weeks until Christmas. What about the store?"

"I've called Don about hiring a university kid for the next few days. And I'll be home by Tuesday night," he promised.

"What about the roads? There's a storm coming in." The drive to Calgary would take between ten to twelve hours, depending on stops and how fast he drove. She hated to think of him making the long trip on his own—especially if the weather turned nasty.

"Roads are great so far." T.J. sounded cheerful. "I'll call you if I run into any problems, but the storm isn't expected until Wednesday."

"Okay."

She hung up the phone, knowing she'd sounded a little petulant. He was doing this for her, because she'd asked him to. At the very least, she could have been more supportive.

But she didn't want him to go *now*. She placed both hands on her stomach. She could feel the muscles grow tight and hard as she experienced one of the mild Braxton-Hicks contractions she vaguely remembered from her first pregnancy.

They'd started early yesterday evening, after her marathon day of baking, shopping and organizing the baby room. Of course, T.J. had been right. It was just too much activity for one day.

She'd make up for it today. Brew a pot of tea and sit on the sofa with a good book. She wouldn't even let herself *think* about the box of Christmas ornaments in the basement.

Heather read for the few hours left of the morning, and drank several cups of tea. By noon she was hungry, but not interested in cooking. She decided to have lunch at the café. She needed to get some fresh air anyway.

She slipped on her wool coat, hat, mitts, boots, and stuffed an extra scarf in her pocket. Bundling up was such an effort, but in these frigid temperatures she couldn't walk even the couple blocks to the café without risking frostbite.

She found the café moderately busy. A group of high school boys hung out at the back, sharing a pizza and taking turns at the video games. Ryan was one of them, but he either hadn't noticed her come in or was choosing to ignore her.

Bernie English and her husband Chad were out with their older daughter, Vicki, and their toddler. Heather stopped at their booth to say hello, and to answer questions about her baby. Yes, she was due shortly, in a couple of weeks as a matter of fact.

She took a booth in the corner, next to the window and settled with a feeling of relief. The short walk had been invigorating but even that small amount of exercise had left her weary.

She picked up the menu from the table from habit, though she already knew what she wanted to eat.

Donna came round and whisked away her coffee mug. "Herbal tea?"

"Not today, Donna. I'm already drowning in the stuff. How about a loaded burger and a chocolate shake? Skip the fries."

"What, you on a health kick?"

"Yeah. Some health kick. Oh, and put extra garlic sauce on my burger, please."

"T.J.'s not planning to sleep with you tonight, I hope."

"Actually, he's gone to Calgary. On business," she added, to forestall any more questions.

She was just finished her meal and counting out money plus tip from the bills in her purse, when a young girl walked into the café.

It was Karen Boychuk, tall and trim in jeans and her caramel-colored sheepskin jacket. People turned their heads, not just the boys at the back, but Donna behind the counter, Bernie, Chad and even Vicki.

There was something so fresh, so lovely, about Karen right now. She was a young woman in her prime—beautiful in a wholesome and natural way. Her appearance on this trying winter day was like brilliant sunshine emerging from behind the clouds after a storm.

Karen seemed unaware of the interest her appearance created. Her gaze flashed from Ryan, to Heather, and back to her boyfriend. She held out her hand in a gesture that told him to wait, then headed for Heather's booth.

"Hi, Karen."

"I thought I saw you in here, Ms. Collins."

"Care to sit down?"

"No. I just wanted to say hi."

She smiled, a little nervously, Heather thought. Karen's gaze swung to the back of the room again. Ryan was obviously waiting for her, his hands on his hips, his face sporting an undisguised scowl.

"I hope you're doing okay, Karen."

"I am, thanks." She set her closed hand on the table, next to Heather's empty glass. "Well, I guess Ryan's waiting for me. I'll see you later." She paused, then added, her voice even softer than before, "Good luck with your baby."

*You, too,* Heather almost said. Instead, she just smiled and nodded. As the young woman turned away, Heather noticed she'd left a slip of paper on the table.

IN YORKTON, T.J. DROPPED off his film at a big chain drug store with one-hour service, then nursed a coffee until the pictures were developed. He put together a package for Sally. The pictures, some of Heather's cookies, the doll clothes he'd found at the store, some cash. Then he took the package to a drop-box for courier pickup. Before letting go of the oversize envelope, he touched his lips to the name printed in bold letters on the front.

"Merry Christmas, Sally."

He returned to his truck, stopped for gas and to check his tires, then headed for the highway. Roads were all clear, driving conditions excellent. He dialed the house and spoke to Heather. After he hung up he realized he'd forgotten to give her his cell phone number.

Oh well, he'd call her tonight and give it to her then.

He leaned back in his seat, popped open the plastic lid on the coffee he'd bought at the gas station and took a quick sip of the scalding liquid. He'd need a lot of this stuff to make the ten-hour drive ahead of him.

After searching the radio for an interesting talk show, he ended up settling on a country music station. The tunes made him think of Heather.

He smiled. He wished this trip was over and he was heading home to her right now. So what if he couldn't tell her how he really felt about her? Being with her was enough. And he didn't want to waste any of the days that were left to them, before the new baby arrived.

But he was doing this because it mattered to her.

He didn't want her to feel ashamed of him, or to have to defend him to her mother or to anyone else.

What he had to do in the next couple days wouldn't give him any pleasure. Macarthur would be crushed, his reputation ruined at the very end of his career. But the clients deserved to know the truth about what had happened to their money.

And he no longer wanted that cloud of culpability hanging over his own head.

Still, as Calgary drew ever closer, T.J.'s dread increased exponentially. He hadn't been back in the city since his divorce. And he'd done his best not to think of the place since.

Not the place and definitely not the people.

Heather had wondered why he hadn't been angry with Lynn and Jeff. Now he wondered, too. He thought about the sitter Lynn had hired every Friday so she could have lunch with the girls. She'd probably been meeting Jeff, instead.

And those nights when he and Jeff would work until midnight, only Jeff would slip out around eight to run to the gym before it closed, well, he'd probably been heading over to T.J.'s house to make out with T.J.'s wife, while T.J.'s daughter slept in the room down the hall.

T.J. sat taller in his seat, hands gripped tightly— oh, so tightly—on the steering wheel.

He still blamed himself, still knew he'd been neglectful, but for the first time he wished that Lynn had at least given him a chance. Sure she'd complained about his outrageous work habits. But she should have let him know the gravity of the situation. If she'd ever said, "Our marriage is on the line here," well, then he'd have been fairly warned, at least.

T.J. was so focused on the past, seeing those years with Lynn from an entirely fresh perspective, that he didn't pay much attention to the radio playing quietly in the background. By supper time, he was about halfway to Calgary. He stopped in Swift Current for gas and a coffee refill. The clerk behind the till asked if he'd heard the revised weather forecast.

"No, what's it say?"

"That the storm they were forecasting for later this week is actually coming in faster than they thought. Now they're expecting it to be here by tomorrow morning. Noon if we're lucky."

MONDAY MORNING HEATHER AWOKE to the radio alarm as usual at seven-thirty. She was just about to force herself out of bed, when a weather advisory came on, followed by an announcement that because of the upcoming storm, public schools were being closed in her district today.

Heather's first thought was for T.J. Was he safely in Calgary? The phone had rung last night, but she'd been in the tub and the answering machine had been off. She hoped he had the sense not to attempt to drive home until after the storm had passed.

Her next concern was for Karen. In her note yesterday, Karen had asked if they could meet at Heather's house on Monday at ten minutes past twelve. She'd intimated that she was worried about her upcoming appointment. And that she needed to talk.

But with this blizzard on its way, and both schools closed, surely Karen wouldn't be coming into town now. All morning Heather expected the phone to ring with a call from either T.J. or Karen. But she heard from neither of them.

Heather made herself tea and sat down with a novel. When she was finished, she looked up at the view from her living-room window. Snow pelted from the sky, driven diagonally across the landscape by gusts of wind.

The storm had arrived.

EARLY MONDAY MORNING T.J. woke up in a motel room just off the highway in Swift Current. First thing he did was turn on the radio and check the forecast. His fears were confirmed—the heavy snowfall and high winds were expected to hit just before noon.

So he had a choice. Push on to Calgary. Or turn back. He was so close to his destination, he hated to give up now. He needed to take care of this Macarthur, Edmond business. It was important to Heather. But the urge to be home with her—*now*—was overpowering. She was three weeks from her due date, but it was possible she could go into labor while he was away. He definitely didn't want that to happen.

Maybe he could leave the file in someone else's hands to take care of. He had a buddy from law school who worked in Swift Current. If it wasn't so early, he'd take Allan Kopchuck the file right now, but the office wouldn't be open for another hour, possibly two. If he waited that long himself, the storm would be right on him.

T.J. decided to think about the problem over a quick breakfast. He checked out of his room and walked across the road to a diner. The place was crowded with men and women who, like him, were reassessing their travel plans. Despite the rush, the middle-aged waitress who took his order was friendly and easygoing.

When he posed his problem, she readily agreed to take care of his file until Allan came to pick it up. Thank God Saskatchewan was still the sort of place where you could trust complete strangers to do something like this for you.

"If anything goes wrong, if my friend doesn't show, you can reach me here, okay?" He scrawled the hardware store's phone number on the back of his bill.

Iris, her name according to the tag pinned above her ample bosom, winked at him. "Wait till my husband hears about this. It's been a few years since one of my customers offered me his phone number."

T.J.'s breakfast bill was under ten dollars. He gave her a fifty. "Let your husband win back your affection by taking you out for lunch on me."

The woman eyed the money suspiciously. "You sure there's nothing illegal going on? This is a heck of a lot of cash for a couple of eggs and holding on to an envelope for a few hours."

"It's perfectly legal," he assured her. "And I should know. I'm a lawyer."

"Oh, heck. And I was really starting to like you."

T.J. grinned "Well, I'm real honored, Iris. It may help to know I'm not actually practicing law at the moment. I own a hardware store. And by holding on to this file for me, you're saving me the gas to drive to Calgary, as well as the cost of lodgings for several nights. So don't feel bad about the money. It's a real deal for me."

Ten minutes later, T.J. was on the road again, headed in the direction he'd come from. He'd let his lawyer friend deal with Macarthur, Edmond. Right now he needed to get back to his wife.

SHORTLY AFTER ELEVEN-THIRTY Heather heard a knock at her front door. She found Karen standing on the stoop. The poor girl's skin was as pale as the snow piling up around her.

"I didn't think you'd come in this weather." Heather closed the door against the force of the wind.

"It's worse out than I thought." Karen shook the snow from her long hair.

"Come in and get warm." Heather took her guest's outdoor clothes and put them on a bench near the hot air register. Hopefully the snow would melt by the time Karen left.

"Would you like something to eat? Or drink?"

Karen wrapped her arms around her middle. Heather wondered if she was imagining a slight thickening of her waist.

"I couldn't eat anything," Karen said. "I'm way too nervous."

"How about a cup of tea, then? I've just put the kettle on."

"Okay."

Karen trailed after Heather into the kitchen. Once they each had a mug of tea in hand, they returned to the living room. Heather's heart ached for the misery she recognized in Karen's face.

She put a sympathetic arm round the young woman's shoulders. "So what's happening?"

"I have my appointment this afternoon." Karen's eyes were huge in her still face. "For the operation. I'm supposed to meet Ryan at the café in half an hour."

She hadn't expected this. "You're sure this is what you want?"

"It'll be easier for everyone. Especially Mom and Dad. This way they'll never have to know anything."

So she still hadn't talked to her parents.

"I know they'd be brokenhearted if they found out," she went on. "Ryan says it'll be kinder this way."

Apparently there weren't any tactics Ryan wouldn't employ to manipulate Karen. Heather, who'd already been struggling to hold a sympathetic view of her former student, found she lost it completely then.

"In one way, yes, I guess it would be kinder. But will you be comfortable keeping something so important from your parents?"

"I don't know." She covered her face with her hands. "Do you think having an abortion is a sin?"

"Oh, Karen. You need to talk to your minister about that. Also, you have to consider your own personal feelings. Will you feel okay having this... procedure...done to your body?"

"I don't see that I have a choice. Ryan is so dead set against anything else."

Heather was truly sick of hearing that young man's name. "Karen, even if you go ahead with this abortion, your relationship with Ryan will never be the same. You'll never go back to the way things were."

Heather could tell Karen didn't want to believe

her. She was clinging to her dream—a dream of marriage and happily ever after with Ryan Farrell.

But from what Heather had been able to observe about Ryan's character—the way he'd responded to his girlfriend's pregnancy, the heavy-duty pressure he was putting on her to have an abortion—Karen's dream had little chance of becoming reality. Even if she did have the abortion, Heather was willing to bet Ryan would break up with her shortly thereafter.

He had his whole life in front of him, after all.

"I want to tell my parents," Karen said softly. "No matter what I decide to do, they deserve to know."

"That's very brave." Heather prayed Mr. and Mrs. Boychuk would stand by their daughter, the way her own parents had done for her.

"As for the abortion…" Karen folded her legs under her and leaned forward, her chin resting on her hands. "I'm still not sure it's right for me. I should have talked to our minister, like you said. But it's too late now. The appointment is today."

"You can always cancel and set another date later if you still want to go ahead with it."

"But you don't know how angry Ryan will be."

"Well, maybe you should—" A heavy knock at the door interrupted her. Heather's first thought was for T.J. Had he been driving in this terrible storm?

She remembered another night, a summer night many years ago. Nick had been on duty. She'd been expecting him home any second. Then she'd heard that knock. And she'd known. She'd *known*.

The distance to her front door felt like the length of a sheet of curling ice. Heather's hand was shaking by the time she reached for the knob.

*Dammit, T.J. If you're dead, I'll never, never forgive you.*

She opened the door.

And for the second time, Ryan Farrell burst into her home uninvited.

## CHAPTER TWENTY

RYAN IGNORED HEATHER, pushed right past her. He marched directly to Karen, grabbed both of her hands and pulled her to her feet. "Lucky thing I saw your truck."

"Ryan, what are you doing here?"

"Bruce was helping me look for you. He dropped me off. We can use your truck to get to Yorkton."

"Are you crazy? You can't just barge into Ms. Collins's house like this."

*"Ms. Collins, Ms. Collins,"* Ryan mimicked in a high-pitched, mocking tone. "She's your hero, isn't she, Karen? Well, I've got news for you. You're not going to have anything more to do with her."

Heather had been trying to hang back in the hall out of his sight. She'd managed to get the phone, was dialing the emergency number, when suddenly Ryan noticed.

"Oh, no, you don't!" He raced for her, knocking the phone out of her hands, almost knocking her to the ground, too.

At that moment of contact, Heather smelled the alcohol on him again. And it was only noon. This kid was out of control, and that scared her. Still, she stood her ground.

"Ryan Farrell, get out of my house. This instant."

He just laughed at her. "And who's going to make me? I know your big, bad husband is in Calgary. I heard you say so at the café yesterday. So who's going to rescue you this time, hey, *teacher?*"

"I can't believe you're acting this way." Karen was on the verge of tears. "You've been drinking, haven't you? Ryan, what in the world is the matter with you?"

"*You're* what's the matter with me, sweetheart." Still holding Heather's phone, he swiveled toward his girlfriend. "Or to be more precise, the little thing growing inside you is the problem. We have to take care of it, Karen. Today. Everything's arranged and I won't let anything—" he glared at Heather "—or *anyone* stop us from taking care of this."

"But Ryan, I'm still not sure this is the right thing for me."

"If I leave this up to you, you'll keep putting off the decision until it's too late. Come on, Karen. You know you don't want to have a baby. You've told me yourself. You've spent half your life looking after your younger brothers. You *deserve* to have some fun and freedom before you have kids. That's what we both deserve."

Heather could see Karen weakening.

"Well, maybe you're right."

"I am. I just wish you could trust me on this."

"I do trust you, Ryan. It's only…" She turned her gaze to Heather, silently beseeching her…for what?

"Ryan, I know you have an important stake in Karen's decision," Heather said. "But you have to accept that this is Karen's decision to make." As soon as she'd made her point, Heather caught her breath. The muscles of her stomach wall were tightening again. Damn, another of those Braxton-Hicks contractions. She'd had a few this morning. But this one had felt strong enough to be a precursor to the real thing.

"Dammit, woman," Ryan said. "Why can't you just stay out of this? It isn't your business."

"You're in my house," she reminded him. "So it *is* my business. What I suggest is that you go home and calm down. You and Karen can talk tomorrow, after she has a chance to speak to her parents and to her minister if she wants to. You can always book another appointment if that's what she decides in the end."

Ryan's eyes blazed with a barely contained fury. "To hell with you and your suggestions."

Heather backed up.

"Come on, Karen." He pulled on his girlfriend's arm, leaving her no recourse but to follow, unless she wanted a dislocated shoulder. "We're going to keep that appointment. Don't listen to anything she says."

Heather couldn't let him leave in this state. Not with Karen. Though she feared for her baby's safety, she blocked the front door with her body.

"You're not taking Karen out of this house, Ryan Farrell. And that's final."

"Is that right?"

She braced herself for a hard shove. Maybe even a blow. But Ryan surprised her by turning very calm. He dropped Karen's hand and took a few steps away from both of them.

"I can see I'll have to switch to Plan B," he said. As Ryan reached for the door handle, Heather rushed to Karen's side.

"Are you okay?" She touched Karen's hand. It was so, so cold.

Then suddenly she realized Ryan hadn't been reaching for the door handle at all. He'd put his hand in the pocket of his jacket. And now he pulled out a gun.

The roughly sawed-off shotgun made her feel faint. She clutched at Karen's arm, as the other girl reached for her, too. Together, they held each other up, as Ryan smiled tightly at the pair of them.

"Okay, Ms. Collins. If you're so worried about Karen leaving with me, why don't you come along and make sure she's all right. Put your coats on, ladies. Don't forget your boots. It's cold out there today."

WITH RYAN'S CRUDE FIREARM pressed to the small of her back, Heather moved with measured steps to Karen's truck. Although Karen had been in her house only half an hour or so, the vehicle was already stone cold. The seat felt like a slab of concrete as Ryan pushed her into the driver's side. He settled in the middle, hauling Karen up next to him with enough force that the young woman yelped with pain. Once the doors were closed, he made sure they were locked.

"Okay, Karen." Ryan sounded calmer now that he had control of the situation. "Give me the keys." He took them, then inserted them in the ignition. "Start the car, Teacher."

Heather was shaking so badly—*from the cold? From fear?*—she could hardly get her fingers around the key. Finally she managed to turn it. The engine made a grinding noise for a few seconds, then started with a loud hum.

"Give it a minute to warm up." Ryan settled into his seat. He put his right arm across Karen's shoulders.

Heather turned slightly, hoping to see how the young woman was doing. She was so quiet, Heather was afraid she might be in shock.

"Just look straight ahead," Ryan told her. "You need to focus on the road in this weather." He glanced over his left shoulder. There were no vehicles coming. No pedestrians, either, unsurprisingly in this weather.

"Okay, you can pull out," he said. "Get on the north road out of town."

That was the way to the Farrell's farm. Was that where he intended to take them?

Heather slipped the automatic transmission into drive. Slowly, the truck rumbled through the drifts of snow. On either side of the road, lights glowed from houses in which families were now eating lunch, watching TV, safely hiding out from the blizzard. Not one of them, she was sure, would ever suspect that one of their neighbors was right this second in a very dangerous situation.

She tried desperately to think of some way to alert them. If she honked her horn, a few might glance out the window. But what would they see? A truck passing by on the road would give no cause for concern. She'd only get Ryan angry.

Which wouldn't be smart.

Right now, the wisest course of action seemed to be to try and talk some sense into the young man.

"Ryan, you're a bright kid. When you were in my class, you were the smartest of the bunch."

The flattery worked. From the corner of her vision, she could see Ryan smile.

"You can do anything with your life, Ryan. And you know it. A guy like you, with lots of smarts and ambition, has to be careful though."

"Don't I know it."

"Think about what you're doing right now. Carrying an illegal weapon. Kidnapping two women. You don't want to get involved with stuff like that."

"I didn't *want* to. Karen gave me no choice." His voice turned petulant. "You know, you were the perfect girlfriend before this happened."

Heather could have screamed.

"You're the prettiest girl in town—no contest. And you're *nice,* too. Every guy in our class wanted you, but I was the only one you ever looked at. I thought we'd go away to university together. That one day we'd get married."

Karen started to cry softly.

"Why did this have to happen?" Ryan sounded as if he suspected Karen of *making* it happen. "And why did you have to be so bloody stubborn about taking care of the problem? I don't see why getting an abortion is such a big deal. How different is it from wearing a condom or being on the pill? Either way, no babies are made. It's the same result."

"Come on, Ryan, you know the issue is much more complicated. The question of when a fetus becomes a human being—"

"Shut up!" Ryan's simmering anger exploded. "This isn't a debating class, *Teacher.* You're screwing with *my life.* Why is that so hard for everyone to understand? Fathers don't have any rights, that's the problem. I am not going to be saddled with support payments before I'm even twenty years old!''

"I wouldn't make you pay if you didn't want to.'' Karen sounded so young, yet determined, too.

"It's not just the money. I don't want the responsibility of a kid.''

"I wouldn't force you to take on that, either.''

"As if I would have any choice. What would people think about a man who turned his back on his own child?''

"Probably no worse than they'd think of a man who forced his girlfriend to have an abortion,'' Heather said.

"Shut up!'' Ryan jabbed his elbow into her arm. Hard.

Heather gasped at the unexpected pain. The truck veered to the left, then to the right as she overcorrected the steering.

"Stay on the goddamned road, would you?''

They were out of town now. Heather could no longer see any lights in the rearview mirror. Although, in this storm, she couldn't see much of anything. Even with the windshield wipers working full tilt she felt like she was inside a snow globe.

The truck was warming up now. Ryan adjusted the heat between defrost and the floor. With him leaning forward, Heather was able to snatch a quick glance at Karen.

She had tears running down her cheeks, and she

shook her head, a silent answer to Heather's unspoken question. So she didn't have any idea what Ryan was up to, either.

At this point, Heather wasn't sure how scared she ought to be. Yes, she'd been abducted at gunpoint, and yes, she was being forced to drive this truck against her will.

But this wasn't a crazy stranger by her side. Sitting next to her, so close their shoulders were in constant contact, was Ryan Farrell, a boy she'd known since he was eight years old. She knew his parents, his two older brothers, too. Ryan *did* have a promising future. He wasn't the kind of kid to stupidly ruin all that.

And yet, he was in the process of doing exactly that.

There had to be some way she could reach him. For his sake, as well as for her and Karen and their babies.

"Ryan, I beg you, please reconsider this. Think about your mother—she's so proud of you. What will she say when she finds out what you've done?"

"She isn't going to find out. Because no one in this truck is going to talk. Get it? Slow down. There's a turn coming up on the right here."

Heather glanced at the odometer. They'd traveled about five kilometers so far. She made the turn off the highway onto a graveled secondary road. She crept up to sixty kilometers an hour.

"You're slower than an ant. Jesus, woman, can't you step on it a little?"

"Not under these conditions, Ryan," she said firmly and thankfully he didn't challenge her. She wondered what he was planning to do once they arrived at his farm. If she remembered correctly, it was up this road a few more kilometers, then a left turn.

But when they reached the intersection she'd recalled, Ryan told her to keep going straight.

"But isn't your farm that way?" she pointed.

"Shut up, I told you!" Ryan slouched back into his seat.

Heather wondered what Karen was thinking. Had she ever seen this side of Ryan before? She must have had glimpses.

Another few minutes passed, then Ryan commanded her again to slow down. He leaned forward in his seat, scanning the landscape anxiously. Heather dared another sideways glance. This time she noticed Karen cupping her wrist with her other hand. She frowned. Had Ryan hurt her? She remembered Karen crying out when he'd forced her into the truck.

That Ryan had been so rough with someone he should care for deeply jacked Heather's fear level up several notches. Just what kind of person *was* Ryan Farrell?

"Okay, this is the corner!" Ryan put a hand on

the steering wheel. Together they maneuvered the truck to the left.

Heather was truly fearful now. This wasn't even a municipally maintained road anymore, just a field access road. The truck had to plow through the snow drifts here, until they came to the edge of a field that in the summer would nurture wheat, or oats, or canola. Now, all Heather could see on the property were a couple of metal granaries, a patchy line of trees along the property line, and lots and lots and lots of snow.

"You can turn around here," Ryan instructed. "Make sure you stay in the tracks or you'll get stuck."

She didn't want to get stuck. Not way out here, miles from the nearest farmhouse. Slowly, cautiously, she circled the truck in the small clearing that Ryan had indicated until the vehicle was pointed in the direction they'd come from.

Heather paused to see what Ryan would want her to do next. She was stunned when all he said was, "Get out."

"What?"

"I said, get out of the truck."

"Are you crazy?" He *had* to be crazy. "I won't last an hour out here." She'd die of exposure. Her *baby* would die, too.

A wild, deep panic exploded inside her. "Ryan this is insane. I'm getting us the hell out of here."

She grasped the steering wheel firmly, then pressed down on the gas. The truck shot forward.

"Like hell!" Ryan slammed his body into her side and grasped the wheel from her control. He forced her over, so she lost control of the accelerator, then stomped on the brake with his left foot.

The truck lurched to a complete stop.

"Get out!" He reached across her body to unlock and then open the driver-side door. Cold air blasted inside the cab.

"Ryan? Please, please don't do this." Karen's voice shook as she pleaded with the boy she'd once thought she loved. Surely now she had to be as afraid and as horrified as Heather.

"I'm begging you. Please let Ms. Collins drive us back to town. I promise I'll get that abortion. I promise I will."

"Damn right you will. Ms. Collin's life depends on it. As soon as you check in at the hospital, I'll drive back here and pick her up. The only way you can make sure your favorite teacher doesn't end up frozen to death is to help me get you into that clinic as fast as possible."

Heather examined Ryan's face carefully. Was he really serious about this crazy plan? "Ryan, it's at least twenty below out here. I'll freeze to death before you get back from Yorkton."

"I've got some blankets in one of the granaries

back there. You'll be okay. If Karen cooperates I can make it back in an hour. What do you say, Karen?''

"Ryan, please…" Tears streamed down Karen's face now. "Please don't leave her here. I *promise* I'll have the operation."

"You've promised before and you always change your mind. I want to be *sure* this time."

"But—"

"Shut up, Karen! Everybody just shut up and do what I say."

Heather knew she was lost now. What were the chances Ryan would come back to get her? Wouldn't it be easier to just leave her here to die? In this storm probably no one had seen the Boychuk's truck. In half an hour, any tire prints would be completely obliterated.

And he'd have the abortion to hold over Karen's head to keep her quiet.

Every way Heather looked at the situation, her best, perhaps her only, chance of survival was to stay in this truck. She grabbed the steering wheel tightly.

"Ryan, let me drive you to the hospital. You heard Karen. She's promised to have the abortion." She slipped her foot sideways, back to the accelerator. Once she had the truck rolling forward, she let go of the wheel with her left hand in order to grab at the open door.

Ryan picked that moment to slam into her again, essentially body-checking her out of the vehicle. As she felt herself slide off the edge of the seat, she grasped desperately for something. Anything.

But she clawed only air as she tumbled to the ground. She grunted as her body first hit, then sank, into a deep bank of snow. She heard Ryan shout an obscenity at her before he slammed the truck door. Ahead of her now, the truck fishtailed, then continued to move, faster and faster. Soon the taillights vanished.

The driving snow created a gray-white cloud that was as effective at obscuring vision as the darkest of nights. Heather swallowed down fear as she realized just how desperate her situation was. Slowly she crawled out of the snowbank, standing tentatively, testing her limbs.

Nothing seemed to be broken or sprained. She was amazed that she'd survived the ordeal as well as she had. She might have a few bruises in her side thanks to Ryan's linebacker tactics, but other than that, she felt fine.

She brushed away as much snow as she could, then pulled in her long wool coat around her. She did up every button and slipped the hood tight around her head. Using the scarf she had in her pocket, she bound the hood in place, protecting her neck, her chin, the entire bottom half of her face, from the elements.

Thank heavens she had warm clothing. Her boots were Sorrels, her mitts were both waterproof and thickly lined. Because the day was so frigid, she'd worn tights under her overalls. And she had a sweater over her long-sleeved T-shirt.

Right now she didn't feel cold at all, but cozy warm, especially when she stood with the wind at her back.

Ruthlessly, she considered her choices for action.

Number one was to stay here and hope Ryan came back for her as he'd said. The downside to this plan was huge. If he didn't return, she would die. No one would drive by this out-of-the-way road for days. And the granary would offer effective protection for only a limited time.

Option number two was to try to make her way to the secondary road where she had at least a hope of flagging down a passing vehicle. If not, she could keep walking to the nearest farm, which she'd clocked on the odometer to be about three kilometers.

Three kilometers wasn't far under most conditions. But here she'd be trudging through deep heavy snow trying to follow a road she couldn't even see. Her biggest risk, she knew, was that she would inadvertently wander off the road into a farmer's field, in which case, she'd be a goner for sure.

She wouldn't be the first unfortunate traveler to meet such a fate. Over the years she'd heard more than a few sad stories about people whose vehicles had broken down on deserted country roads. The conventional wisdom was that during extremely cold weather or a blizzard, you were better off to stay with your disabled vehicle than attempt to walk for help.

But she didn't have a vehicle so she didn't have that choice. Really, the only sensible thing to do was to walk. At least by moving she could help keep her body warm.

Following in the path of the truck that had just left her behind, Heather struck a determined pace. If only this damn storm would stop. She wouldn't have a clue where to go once the truck tracks were snowed in.

## CHAPTER TWENTY-ONE

HEATHER WASN'T HOME WHEN T.J. arrived back in Chatsworth, even though the lights were on and the front door unlocked. He noticed the carpet was wet in the living room. The whole scene seemed off-kilter somehow.

He dialed Adrienne, then Heather's mom and everyone else she might be visiting. He came up with no answers at all.

Two mugs were on the coffee table, both half full of herbal tea that was now cold, although the pot on the stove still felt slightly warm. He examined the mugs closely. One had traces of the pink lipstick Heather favored. The other had lipstick, too, though a darker shade.

He checked the closet next. Heather's coat and boots were missing. But her car was still parked in the garage at the back of the house, her keys hung on a hook next to her purse. She wouldn't have walked far in this weather. And he'd already called all her friends who lived nearby.

Where the hell could she be?

He wanted to phone the police, but was sure his

concerns wouldn't be taken seriously. He returned to the landing at the front door and looked at the concrete stoop. Here the overhanging roof protected the walk from the majority of the snowfall, but the wind had sent a dusting of powder over the area. On close examination, he saw the remains of tracks that were older than his fresh ones.

He recognized the pattern of Heather's boots leaving the house and eliminated those. That left two other patterns. Both had walked into the house and back out again. One set was pointy-toed, about the same size as Heather's. The other was larger, with a tread like a running shoe.

T.J. revised the scene he'd imagined earlier. The woman had come first, otherwise there would have been three mugs on the table, not just two. The man had arrived later, interrupting their conversation, possibly walking in with snow on his shoes, just like...

Oh, man. Goddammit, no! He'd *promised* Heather he wouldn't let that kid bother her again. But Ryan Farrell must have been here. Nothing else made sense. T.J. thought back to the night he'd had to forcibly remove Ryan from this house. He should have pulverized the snotty kid when he had the chance.

He'd let Heather down—big time. And now he had no idea where she was, or even if she was okay. The other woman she'd had tea with must have been Ryan's girlfriend—Karen Boychuk. Was Heather with Ryan and Karen now? But where could they be?

T.J. decided to start with Karen's family. Maybe they had some idea where he could find their daughter—and by extension, his wife, too.

Karen's mother answered his call on the first ring. She told him that her daughter had borrowed their truck without asking. They'd only just realized it was missing. She assumed Karen had gone out to meet her boyfriend, Ryan Farrell.

"I'm a little worried with this storm, though," Mrs. Boychuk confessed. "I hope she'll call home soon."

So did T.J. He dialed the Farrell's next and spoke to Abe who had seen Ryan leave with his friend Bruce. T.J. asked for that phone number and was soon speaking to the eighteen-year-old.

"Ryan saw Karen's truck at your place." Bruce told him. "He asked me to drop him off and I haven't heard from him since."

T.J. was stymied. He simply couldn't think of the next logical step to take. Why would Heather have left the house with Ryan and Karen? Where could they possibly have gone? He wanted to go out searching, but had no idea where to start. Besides, if he went out, he might miss her call if she happened to make one.

But why would she when she thought he was on

his way to Calgary? Oh, God, he should have given her his cell phone number long ago.

T.J. paced from the living room to the front door, stopping to check anxiously out the window every time. *Come on, Heather. Where are you?*

It seemed like an hour passed, though it was probably only ten minutes since he'd made his last call, when the phone finally rang. T.J. dashed across the room to answer before the second ring.

"Hello?"

"T.J.? This is Karen's mother. We just—we just had a very s-strange call from our daughter."

T.J. had to struggle to hear. The line wasn't a good one, and the woman was so upset she could barely talk. Something was seriously wrong.

"Where is she? Is Heather with her?"

"Karen's at the hospital in Yorkton. My husband and I are on our way now. She said Ryan Farrell tried to force her to—to have an *abortion.*"

She started to cry then, leaving T.J. in complete frustration. *Where is Heather?*

Mr. Boychuk took control of the phone. "T.J.? Karen said Ryan blamed Heather—for what I have no idea. I guess he thought Heather was preventing Karen from doing what he wanted her to do." The poor man paused for a moment, then gamely continued. "Karen says Ryan forced Heather to drive out into the country. Then he kicked her out of the truck in the middle of nowhere and carried on taking Karen to the clinic.''

''You mean he just *left* her? Outside, in the blizzard?''

''I'm afraid so. You'll have to find her fast. We called the police before we called you, but you know the countryside better than they will.''

''Any idea where Farrell left her?''

''Karen said it was a farm access road a couple kilometers past the turnoff to the Farrells' farm.''

''The quarter-section he seeded with flax last year?''

''That's the one.''

T.J. knew it. In good weather he could drive there in under fifteen minutes. How long would it take him tonight?

''Okay, thanks. I'm going to look for her right now.''

''Good luck.''

Poor Mr. Boychuk sounded lost as he said that. T.J. spared a second of sympathy for the couple who'd just found out in the most shocking way possible that their teenaged daughter was pregnant. But only a second. His pregnant *wife* was outside in this blizzard somewhere.

How could Farrell do that? Leave a helpless, pregnant woman out on the Saskatchewan prairie in a snowstorm... Would the cold put Heather's pregnancy at risk? T.J. was afraid that might be of secondary concern now. How long had Heather been out in the cold? How much longer could she last?

He tried calling the Farrells', but couldn't get through this time. Maybe the phone lines were down thanks to the storm.

Abandoning the phone, T.J. gathered a flashlight, filled a thermos with hot water, grabbed a pile of wool blankets from the linen cupboard. He raced out to his truck, throwing the stuff onto the passenger seat as he slid behind the wheel. Before he'd even had a chance to shut the driver-side door, he took off, heading for the north exit from town.

Traffic was nonexistent along the highway. He passed a few cars stuck in the ditch. T.J. watched closely for the first turnoff. Once he'd made that, he pushed his truck for as much speed as he dared. All the while he kept reminding himself to be careful.

He wouldn't be much help to Heather if he landed in the ditch himself.

HEATHER FELT LIKE SHE'D BEEN walking for hours, but according to her watch it had been about fifty minutes. She battled the wind coming at her from the side, bringing a constant buffeting of snow—not flakes, but hard pebbles of ice that stung against her cheek. She felt as if she'd never worked harder in her life, but with precious little progress.

Despite all her walking, there were still no farm buildings in sight. Either she was moving slower than she figured, or she'd underestimated the distance to the Farrell's homestead. Maybe she should have taken shelter in that granary…

She no longer felt warm, but was freezing cold. She'd withdrawn her thumbs from the separate compartments in her mitts so she could clench her hands in fists for extra warmth. Even so, her fingers were growing numb.

Already she'd lost feeling in her toes. And the tip of her nose. She tried to keep the scarf over most of her face, but it kept slipping down.

With every gust of wind, she felt a chill travel across her shoulders and down her back. Her body shivered uncontrollably and she worried what effect this might have on the baby. She clutched both arms around her middle as she stumbled forward.

*T.J., where are you now?* She hoped he'd arrived safely in Calgary and was at this very moment showing his file of information to someone who would make sure the truth was revealed.

She found it helped to imagine him beside her, urging her on. He'd be a tyrant, of course, saying things like, *Can't you move any faster?* Or, *Take it out of reverse, Beatrice.*

Beatrice. She wondered if she'd ever hear him call her that again. Wondered if she'd ever see him, or *anyone* she loved again.

Because she did love him. Not the warm, steady, safe love she'd had for Russell. No, this was something rawer, more primal, intensely elemental. There'd been a reason she and T.J. had struck sparks against each other from kindergarten on. Now she understood.

T.J. had always been the one to help her out of the worst messes in her life—not with grace, mind you, but still, he hung in there when the going was tough.

While Russell never had. Not with her, anyway.

*Oh, T.J.* There were so many things she needed to tell him. Now she'd probably never have the chance. The possibility of that—that she would die and he would never know how she'd felt about him—finally brought on the tears. She indulged herself for a minute or so, then regained control through sheer determination.

She had to focus what little energy she had left on keeping her baby alive, on keeping her feet moving, on keeping her wits about her.

But, oh, Lord, she was so cold.

WHEN T.J. PASSED THE TURNOFF to the Farrell farm, he eased off the accelerator. He knew the farm access road was coming up and he didn't want to miss it. It would be an easy mistake to make in these conditions.

Oh, God, if it would only stop snowing. Was that too much to ask?

Apparently so, because the stuff kept dumping

from the sky as if God was determined to bury all of Saskatchewan in the space of this one bitter day.

Eventually T.J. saw it—the rise in the ditch that signaled an intersecting road. Carefully, he took the corner. Track marks from an earlier vehicle were almost completely blown over. He had to focus all his attention on the road to follow them.

He drove one achingly slow kilometer. Then a flash of red in the snow had him hitting the brakes and almost losing control of his truck. As soon as he had the truck stopped, he leapt from his seat to investigate.

He found a long red scarf, already partially covered in new snowfall. Another ten or fifteen minutes and it might have been completely buried.

It was Heather's scarf.

SHE WASN'T COLD ANYMORE. No, she was deliciously warm and happy, because wasn't that her house just up ahead by that tree? Funny, she'd thought Ryan had made her drive so far into the country, but really they'd been here in Chatsworth all this time.

T.J. would be home waiting for her. He'd make her tea and give her a bath. She wanted to see him so very, very badly.

But maybe she should take just a tiny little rest first. She'd been walking for so long and she was so tired.

At least she wasn't cold anymore. She'd gotten rid of her restrictive scarf earlier, and now she unbuttoned the top half of her coat.

Look at all the beautiful snowflakes. They'd have a white Christmas this year, all right. She couldn't wait to go to church with T.J. on Christmas Eve. Singing carols was one of her favorite holiday activities.

"Fa la la la la," she sang now, just for the joy of hearing her voice. She couldn't understand why she'd been so worried earlier. Everything was going to be okay, she knew it was.

Another one of the cramps hit her, and she paused, putting her hand to the small of her back. There was something important about what she was feeling right now. She knew she'd felt something like it before. If she could only remember...

Oh, the pain was getting worse. Maybe she should just lie down until the feeling passed. She bent her knees slightly, then her body just seemed to melt on top of the snow.

Heather rested her cheek against a pillow of snow. This was so comfortable. She should have tried this much earlier.

Maybe she'd have a nap, just a very short one. And then she'd go home and be with T.J.

"HEATHER! HEATHER! HEATHER!" T.J. hollered the name into the howling wind, as he battered his way through knee-high snowdrifts, following the path of broken snow. He could see no sign of her ahead.

Fear had him moving as fast as he could. She couldn't be too far away or the scarf wouldn't have been visible anymore.

How had she—eight and a half months pregnant—managed to plow through all this snow? And why had she veered off the road? She must have become disoriented. Not a good sign. How long had she been out in this cold? He calculated just over an hour. He had to find her. He had to. How much farther could she be? He was moving as fast as he could, damn it, and he just couldn't seem to...

He caught a glimpse of something black in the snow in front of him. Heather's coat was black, but maybe he'd just seen a shadow in the snow. A few seconds later, though, he saw a slight movement.

He felt like he was in one of those bad dreams, when you wanted to run, but couldn't. This damn snow! ''Heather? Heather?''

He heard the faintest of sounds in return.

''Heather, don't worry. I'm almost there!'' He redoubled his efforts but he was already moving as fast as physically possible. As he drew near, he heard the sound again. It sounded like singing.

And then again, feeble and off-key, but definitely a song, ''Deck the halls with...''

Finally he was there! ''Heather? Sweetheart?'' He

plucked her out of the snow. Her eyes were open, but didn't focus on him correctly.

"What took you so long?" she said. "I want to decorate the Christmas tree."

"Later," he promised as he propped her up as best he could, while wrapping one of the wool blankets tightly around her.

"What are you doing? I don't need that." She batted her hands ineffectively against the blanket.

Heather looked and sounded drunk, but T.J. knew disorientation was a symptom of hypothermia. He tried not to worry about whether her core temperature had lowered enough to harm the baby. Right now he needed to focus on saving the mother, saving his wife.

Once he had her wrapped up, he whisked her into his arms, carrying her like a baby. This wasn't the first time he'd picked her up, but in winter gear, with all this snow to work against, the effort was much more difficult.

He huffed as he struggled to put one foot ahead of the other.

"Th-e firrr-st No-o-el," Heather sang, drawing out each slurred word.

"Hush, baby, I'm going to take care of you. Don't you worry."

They were almost back to the point where he'd found the scarf, when Heather suddenly moaned in pain.

"What? Did I hurt you?" And when she didn't stop. "Heather, are you okay?"

"My stomach," she finally gasped. She'd let go of his neck to clutch her middle.

It took a few seconds for T.J. to realize what was happening.

His wife was in labor.

## CHAPTER TWENTY-TWO

T.J. WAITED OUT HEATHER'S contraction, then continued his desperate efforts to get his wife to his truck. He held her close as he struggled through the snow, muttering encouragement that might have been directed to her or to himself, he wasn't sure which.

"Hang in there, sweetheart. Good thing you're such a little thing. We're almost there. Here's where I found your scarf. There's the truck, can you see it through all this blowing snow?"

He propped her up against the passenger-side door, then yanked open the driver door to start the ignition and warm up the engine. Running back to Heather, he brushed the snow off her coat and mitts and pulled off her boots to make sure her feet were dry.

He wrapped her in two of the dry blankets from the truck then settled her in the center of the bench seat, buckling her seat belt with great effort.

"Stop bothering me!" She swatted at his hands. "Can't you just leave me alone?"

He opened the thermos of hot water and poured some into a plastic cup. "Can you drink this, Heather?"

Her disorientation had him deeply worried. Once she'd had some of the warm liquid, he scrambled into the driver's side and took off for the main road. He had to get her to the hospital and quickly. Using his cell phone he called ahead to let the emergency department know to expect them. No sense sending an ambulance, he'd get her there faster.

When warm air began wafting out of the vehicle's heating system, he turned the fans to high and soon the cab was uncomfortably warm for him, but he knew Heather needed the heat.

"Heather? How are you feeling?" He wanted to get her talking.

"That water was good."

"There's more in the thermos. Can you help yourself?"

She tried, but her hands were stiff and she spilled onto the seat. "Sorry, T.J."

"It doesn't matter, sweetheart. All that matters is getting you warm again. Can you feel your toes?"

"They hurt, T.J. My fingers, too." Heather forgot about the water as she groaned with the pins-and-needles pain of the returning blood flow to her extremities.

Then she had another contraction, and almost fell apart completely. "Make it stop, T.J.! Make it stop!"

Oh, he wished he could help her. "I'll get you to the hospital as fast as I can." He turned right onto the municipal road, and found the driving conditions worse than before. His earlier tracks were snowed in and with the windshield battered by falling snow, he could hardly see. The headlights shone valiantly ahead, but discerning where the road ended and the ditch began was nearly impossible. He steered more on instinct than anything else.

"I'm so tired." In between contractions, Heather tried to curl up on the seat, but her belt prevented her.

"Leave that on, please," T.J. begged, as Heather tried to unfasten the seat belt. "I'm trying like hell to keep us out of the ditch, but if anything happens, you have to be wearing that."

"I'm so tired," she repeated.

"I know, sweetheart. But you need to stay awake. Okay? We've got to get you to hospital. I think you're going to have our baby tonight."

"Our baby," she repeated, letting her head droop over to his shoulder.

He put a hand on her thigh, wishing he could hold her close. "I love you so much. You know that, right?"

"Love you," she repeated again, this time snuggling even closer.

He needed to keep her awake, and so he continued to talk. "You've always fascinated me, right from when we were kids. Your red hair and pretty smile and most of all, that glow you've always had. What is it, Heather? What makes you so happy?

When she didn't answer, he glanced sideways to make sure she wasn't sleeping. Her eyes were open. Huge. And staring right at him.

"When we were kids I knocked myself out trying to win your attention. I know I tormented you at times. But really, deep down, I wanted to be your friend. Later, when we were older, I wanted a hell of a lot more."

Funny how easy it was to tell her all this right now. They were in their own little world. From the cozy warmth of the truck cab, the view of the storm outdoors seemed surreal.

"The day we were married, I knew I finally had everything I'd ever really wanted. But I was so scared I was going to screw it up. The way I did with Lynn."

"No, T.J.," she protested mildly.

He wasn't sure what she meant. Wasn't sure she was even following the conversation. Still, he kept talking.

"I know I held back when you were doing your best to be a loving wife. I'm sorry if I hurt you, Heather. I was just so afraid that you would never love me the way you loved Russell. I figured it was better if I never even tried to measure up to him."

"Oh, T.J."

She was beginning to sound more like herself. Was she warming up, then? Would she be okay?

They had reached the turnoff to the highway. T.J.

paused at the stop sign, before merging onto the semideserted roadway. In the distance, he saw one set of faint taillights, that was all.

At least here there were tracks in the snow to follow. He didn't have to worry about veering into the wrong lane or off into the ditch. He increased speed, as Heather was racked by another contraction. They were about seven minutes apart, he figured. Hopefully he'd get her to the hospital in time. But would there be any permanent damage from the hypothermia? T.J. worried about both his wife and his baby.

"Hang in there sweetheart. I'm going as fast as I dare."

ONCE T.J. DROVE UP TO the emergency wing of the Yorkton Union Hospital, he was glad to let the trained personnel take charge of the situation. Heather was given priority treatment, encased in a special warm-air circulating blanket, given more warm liquids to drink. An IV was started, to pump warm fluids through her system and thus raise her core temperature more quickly.

She seemed a little bewildered, but basically herself. Still, T.J. worried. "Is she going to be okay?"

The ER doctor gave him a reassuring nod. "She's responding well to treatment and we've got the baby's heart rate up from 130 to 150." He perched on the edge of a chair on rolling wheels and wheeled closer to Heather's side. "Can you tell me what happened?"

Heather glanced at T.J. mutely. He guessed she was either too exhausted, or too upset to answer the question. Holding her hand tight in his, he recounted the events as far as he knew, without explaining why Heather was out in the storm in the first place.

"Sounds like you did all the right things," the doctor told T.J. He was in his mid-forties, with a reassuring calmness that T.J. appreciated.

"My wife was pretty out of it when I first found her."

"That's normal, even for cases of mild hypothermia. The important thing is that you got her into a dry, warm environment. Drinking hot water was a good idea, too. Much better than the tea or coffee people often make the mistake of administering."

The doctor rolled his chair back toward the door, removed his rubber gloves.

"So what happens now?" T.J. wondered anxiously. He wrapped his arm around Heather, whom he could tell was enduring another contraction, though she hadn't uttered a word of complaint.

The doctor smiled. "We send your wife to the OB ward. The warm IV may have slowed her labor a little, but still I think it's time for her to have this baby."

"T.J.!" HEATHER GRABBED HER husband's arm urgently. They were walking the hospital corridors as she endured the prolonged first stage of her labor. "You need to find Karen Boychuk. Ryan's trying to force her to have an abortion."

Heather couldn't believe she'd forgotten. Something strange had happened to her mind when she was out in the storm. She remembered the cold, how tired she had felt. Maybe she'd fallen asleep, because she thought she'd dreamed about Christmas.

Only vaguely could she recall T.J. finding her, then carrying her back to his truck. She was amazed he'd been able to do that. Sure, he'd hauled her off to the bedroom a few times, but tonight she'd been wearing all that winter gear, plus he'd had the snow to struggle with, too.

Somehow he'd done it, though. He'd gotten her to safety, to this hospital. And she'd been so confused and worried for their baby, that for a while she'd forgotten why all of this had happened in the first place.

"Don't worry about Karen. She managed to phone her parents before anything happened."

"Thank God." She shared a smile with her husband. She'd been pretty confused when he'd been driving her to Yorkton, but she remembered some of what he'd said to her on the way. She was almost certain he'd told her he loved her. More than once.

His heroic efforts to save her, his attentiveness now, proved it.

"I'm so glad you turned back and came home." She squeezed his arm.

"Me, too. What happened, Heather? I got to the house around one o'clock." He told her about piecing together a story based on the footprints he saw on the front walk and the two mugs he found in the living room.

"You've pretty much figured out the whole story, Sherlock." Her teasing smile faded as another contraction began to build. She stopped walking and gripped T.J.'s hand tighter.

He coached her through it like an old pro. And soon she was able to talk again.

"Karen came over around noon to talk to me. She had an operation to terminate the pregnancy booked for this afternoon. I think she wanted me to talk her out of going, but we didn't get a chance to finish our conversation. She'd only been at my place about half an hour when Ryan Farrell showed up."

T.J. swore.

"He had a gun, T.J. He'd sawed the barrel off an old shotgun. He forced Karen and me into her father's truck, then he made me drive out to that field."

"Stupid kid. You can bet he's in serious trouble now."

"I felt sorry for him before, but no longer," Heather had to confess. "Poor Karen. She had herself convinced he was her prince charming. She must be so upset right now."

"Trust you to worry about someone else when you're in the middle of having a baby. Do me a favor, Heather?"

"For you? Just about anything."

"Just about?"

"I know how outrageous you can be."

"True." He held her close. "But not today. Today I'm Mr. Sane and Serious. All I want is for you to concentrate on having this baby. Let's worry about Karen another time."

THEODORE JACKSON COLLINS was born at seven o'clock on Tuesday morning, three weeks before his due date, almost two weeks before Christmas.

"We're going to have to put up a Christmas tree after all," Heather said. The nurse had placed their naked baby on Heather's bare skin. Heather held him close so that his pursed mouth was right next to one of her nipples. Though she kept offering him something to drink, he seemed determined not to accept.

"What are you talking about?" T.J. had hoped they could skip all that fuss. He had enough with decorating the store, let alone their home, too.

"I wasn't going to bother before. But this will be Teddy's first Christmas. I want it to be perfect."

"Like the kid's going to notice."

"That isn't the point."

T.J. sighed. Not unhappily. "I guess I can string

up a few more strands of lights if it makes you happy.''

"It will,'' she promised. The baby made some rooting movements, and she offered him her nipple. Again, the kid just couldn't seem to get the right idea.

"Is this normal?'' T.J. asked the next nurse who checked up on them.

"Happens all the time,'' she said, bending over Heather to offer more instruction. "Breastfeeding doesn't always come as easily as we expect it to.''

"But he *will* figure this out eventually, won't he?'' Wetness glimmered in Heather's eyes.

This was clearly very important to her. T.J. could guess why. After the nurse had made her reassuring noises and left, he leaned in close to his wife.

"Do you mind that he's a boy?''

She frowned, then regarded him closely. "You mean because of Jason?''

She said the name easily, as if it caused her no pain. "Yeah. Because of Jason.'' He'd been hoping for a girl for that very reason.

"I'm fine, T.J. Don't worry. I don't feel badly about Jason. In my heart I know he was meant to end up with the family he has. They're very happy together. And as for this little one—'' she ran a finger down the side of the baby's reddened cheek "—I think it's perfect that he's a boy. Except for having to name him Theodore Jackson, of course.''

T.J. was used to seeing Heather blush. But now he felt his own skin turn warm. "I hated those names when I was a kid. I always swore I'd never do that to my kid if I ever had a boy."

"They're fine names, T.J. I was just teasing you. I'm glad you're carrying on the family tradition. It'll mean a lot to your mom and dad."

"You think?"

"I do."

Her tender smile reminded him of all the reasons he loved her. Then she turned her head down to the baby again.

"Look at that, T.J.," Heather breathed quietly.

While they'd been discussing his new names, their son had finally latched on. As Heather cuddled him closer, he took his first instinctive sucks.

"I think this is the happiest moment of my life," Heather said.

T.J. knew it was his.

## CHAPTER TWENTY-THREE

THE NEXT DAY HEATHER'S hospital room was party central. First came her parents. T.J. had called Marion and Ron the previous night and they were anxious to see for themselves that Heather truly had survived her horrible ordeal unscathed. And of course they were dying to meet their new grandson.

"Oh, look at all this fuzz!" Marion cuddled the baby in her arms and brushed the top of his head gently with one finger. "That's how your hair looked when you were born, Heather."

Heather grinned. Her sparkling eyes met her husband's. T.J. had been hovering at her bedside all night. She didn't think he had slept a wink.

"So, T.J.," she said. "How do you feel about your son having *red* hair? Sounds like poetic justice to me."

He touched the side of her face tenderly. "Right now, nothing could faze me. We can think about transplant therapy later."

Heather laughed and so did her parents. Her dad nudged her mother. "Planning to hog that baby all morning? Doesn't Granddad get a turn?" Heather loved seeing her parents fuss over the new baby. They had waited a long time for this moment. They deserved every bit of their happiness.

And she felt better knowing that her baby had all these people who loved him. When T.J.'s parents returned from their trip—they'd committed to March when T.J. had called them to announce Teddy's arrival—they'd be doting grandparents, too, she was sure. Her child would grow up with a secure family base of support. Something she hadn't been able to offer Jason years ago. She was so glad she'd found a family that could.

Her father, now holding the new infant confidently in his arms—weren't men supposed to be scared of newborn babies?—came and sat on the edge of her bed.

"We're so happy for you, sweetheart." He kissed her forehead.

"Thanks, Dad. I'm pretty happy, too."

"You look great. No side effects from what happened last night?"

She shook her head. "No. The doctors say I'm just fine."

"Thank you, T.J., for rescuing our Heather for us." Ron's eyes were teary as he acknowledged his son-in-law. "I still can't believe one of Abe Farrell's sons could do something like that."

"Yes, thank you, T.J." Marion gave him a kiss on the cheek and a tight hug. "We talked to the police last night. You really downplayed your role, but when the constable told us how far you carried Heather through the snow, we couldn't believe it was possible.''

''I had a lot at stake,'' T.J. said. ''Kind of gives a man motivation.''

Just then a suspicious sound came from the baby. Everyone laughed, and Heather joked to her father, ''You're holding him, Dad. The diapers are over there.'' She pointed to the plastic cot where the baby was meant to sleep, only he hadn't been put in there once.

Ron wrinkled his face. ''I don't know, Heather...''

''I'll do it.'' T.J. took tender hold of his infant son. ''I've had some practice already. I think I'm getting pretty good at this.'' He winked at his wife.

Heather was reminded of something he'd said when they'd first found out she was pregnant. That he could count on one hand the number of times he changed Sally's diaper. Looked like he was determined to be a different kind of father for Teddy.

A tap sounded at the partially closed door. At Heather's invitation, Karen Boychuk stepped tentatively into the room. She wore jeans and a jacket over her shoulders. Her left arm was in a sling.

''Oh, Ms. Collins.'' She seemed almost too overwhelmed for words. She looked from her teacher, to the baby T.J. was carefully administering to, while his father-in-law watched.

"The trick is to make sure it's pointed down before you do up the Velcro," T.J. said.

Ron nodded sagely.

Heather smiled at her former student. "I think after all we've been through together, we should be on a first-name basis."

"Yes, I think you're right, *Heather.*" She added the Christian name a little self-consciously. "I heard you had a baby boy. He looks perfect."

"Yes, he is." Heather's heart ached as she saw the mixture of longing and pain in Karen's eyes as she watched the baby. "How are you? Is your wrist broken?"

"Sprained." Her lower lip trembled. She struggled not to cry. "I'm so sorry, Heather."

Heather's parents stepped to the side with T.J. and the baby, giving the two women an opportunity to say what needed to be said.

"Karen, you have nothing to be sorry about."

"I knew he didn't want me to see you. I should never have come to your house yesterday. What if something had happened to your baby when you were out in that field? What if something had happened to *you?*"

"It was a scary experience," Heather admitted. "But none of it was your fault. Please don't ever feel that it was." She hesitated before asking, "Have you heard about Ryan?"

Karen's gaze dropped to the floor. "He's in custody right now. The police caught up to him about a kilometer past his farm. For what it's worth, he *was* going back to get you. Dad says charges are pending. They think there's a good chance Ryan will spend at least some time in jail.''

*Good,* Heather felt like saying. She realized now, too late, that she should have pressed charges the first time Ryan had stepped out of line. Maybe she could have prevented him from this latest, most desperate mistake.

''I feel so deceived. I really thought he was the greatest guy.''

''Ryan has a lot going for him,'' Heather conceded. ''Something inside him just snapped. I hope he gets the help he needs. But now you have to focus on what *you* need. So how are you doing? And what about your parents—are they as upset as you were afraid they'd be?''

''They're still in shock, I think. But they've been a lot nicer than I expected. Mom told me this morning that they'll go along with whatever I decide about the baby.''

''I'm so glad.''

''Apparently my aunt and uncle in Edmonton have always wanted a child. It's possible I might go to school there after all. We'll work out something for the baby…'' Her gaze traveled to Heather's infant again, who was now being held by his daddy. ''I wish I could give him everything that *your* baby has.

A mom and a dad and…'' She paused, again struggling for control.

Heather reached out her hand. ''It's okay, Karen. I know how you feel right now. Like your life is off track and it can never be put right again. But it can. You will get through this.''

''You think?''

''Just look at me. I'm the perfect example.''

HEATHER AND THE BABY WERE discharged the next day. On their way home, they stopped at her parents' farm for lunch and ended up staying until early evening. It was seven o'clock and dark by the time they were on the road again. Within minutes, T.J. spotted the small scattering of lights that was Chatsworth.

He turned left just past the grain elevator, stopped to check both ways before crossing the railway tracks, then paused at the intersection of Willow Road and Lakeside Drive.

His usual route home would take them right past the Matthews' new house. A place he'd rather avoid right now. But if he took an alternate way home, wouldn't Heather wonder? And he couldn't avoid the specter of Russell Matthew forever, anyway.

He stayed on Lakeshore, driving slowly as Heather exclaimed over all the pretty Christmas lights. When they came to the Matthews' place, she fell silent. He felt compelled to pause the vehicle and look, too.

White fairy lights outlined the old-fashioned front

porch, the massive wood door was decorated with an unbelievably beautiful wreath. T.J. could almost smell hot apple cider wafting along with the scent of smoked birch from the billowing chimney.

"Tasteful and elegant as always," was Heather's comment.

"Yeah." He wondered if there'd been any envy behind her words. He wondered if she still wished she was the woman living in that house. That this was the *second* son she was bringing home to Russ.

He pulled away from the curb, took another left, headed for home.

He *should* have driven another route if he was going to torture himself by thinking this way. Maybe he hadn't been Heather's first choice, but he had her now, didn't he? He'd be smart to make the best of his good fortune.

"Let's drive down Main Street, too, T.J.," Heather suggested. "The baby's still sleeping—we don't need to rush. I want to see the lights at the hardware store. Maybe we'll have time to decorate our house tomorrow."

Obligingly T.J. toured slowly along the main street of town. Most merchants had decorated for the holidays, but few to the degree of his store.

"The hardware looks great," Heather said.

"Thanks to Don. He always goes a little crazy when he sees the holiday stock come in. He claims the products sell better if we display them at the store.'' Probably Don was right, because Christmas sales had been very good this year.

Heather sighed. She sounded happy. ''Let's go home now.''

He U-turned at the war memorial, then headed back to Mallard Avenue. A few of the houses along the way had a single strand of lights along their roof lines. A couple had also decorated one or two of the smaller trees in their front yard.

Then they came to their house, where multicolored lights danced along the roof and windows and also up and around a thirty-foot spruce. Looking at it now, comparing it with the Matthews', T.J. wondered if it wasn't just a little bit overdone.

Heather didn't seem to think so, though. ''Oh, I love it! Thank you, T.J. This is the best surprise ever!'' She rushed out of the front seat and stood on the sidewalk with her hands clasped together. Tipping her head back, she let her gaze focus on the very top of the big spruce.

''How did you get the lights way up there?''

''I used a metal pole with a hook on the end. And a very tall ladder.'' He stood slightly behind her, still anxious. Did Heather really like it?

They heard a tiny squeak from the car, and Heather rushed to get the baby. T.J. carried in the assorted paraphernalia: Heather's bag and the flowers he'd bought for her and the supplies they'd purchased for the baby at the drug store on their way out of town.

Once inside, the first thing Heather noticed was the Christmas tree T.J. had bought yesterday, after he did the lights.

"I didn't decorate it," he said. "I thought maybe you'd like for us to do that together."

"Where did you find the time? Oh, T.J. this is all so perfect. I can't tell you how happy you've made me."

"You wouldn't have preferred white lights outside?" *Like the Matthews'…?*

"No. I love all the colors. I do." She took his hands, then pulled him close and kissed him, soft and sweet. "Let me feed the baby. Then we need to talk."

T.J. DID THE UNPACKING while Heather fed the baby. When she was done, she carried Teddy, sleeping against her shoulder, into the living room. She found T.J. adding water to the tree. He'd lugged up her box of ornaments from the basement and had already strung the lights on the tree. While she settled on the sofa, he plugged them in.

"Oh!" She supposed it was childish of her. But she really did love Christmas lights.

T.J. went around the house, flicking off all the other lights, adding to the magical effect of their first

Christmas tree. When he was done, she patted the cushion next to her. "Come sit here."

She loved the way he snuggled in close and put an arm around her and the baby. She had so much she wanted to tell him, but he was the first to talk.

"You know, Heather, if you'd like a new house, we could certainly afford to build one. I saved most of my salary when I was working in Calgary—Lynn and I lived pretty economically. So I have a nest egg built up."

That explained his investment accounts. But why would he think she wanted a new house? "I like our place. Isn't it big enough for you?"

"I think it's great. I just wondered if you would like something…grander."

"Not at all."

She sensed the question in his eyes as he looked at her so deeply. She knew it really wasn't the house he was wondering about at all.

"I've gone a lot of years pining after Russell Matthew. I thought he was the perfect man for me. I never believed I'd love anyone as much as I loved him."

T.J. continued to watch her. He didn't say anything, but his gaze told her that every word she said mattered to him.

"But I realized something the night I was walking by myself in that field. Before my mind started to go a little crazy, I was thinking about my past, about you and me in particular.

"You used to drive me crazy, T.J., but I think it's because you triggered feelings that I was afraid to acknowledge. In many ways, being with Russ was easier. Our relationship gave me the perfect excuse to keep you at a distance."

"What are you saying?"

"That it's you, not Russ, that my heart belongs to. Last night, when I thought I might die, I was really, really angry about all the wasted years. If I hadn't been such a coward, we might have been together ages ago."

T.J.'s arm around her tightened. "I love you so much, Heather. I've always loved you."

"I know that now. And I love you, too."

His lips sought hers for a slow, exploratory kiss. They were both very careful not to wake the baby lying between them.

"I'll never forget how you looked at our high school grad. You had such a glow about you. I think that's the first time I realized I wanted to marry you."

"In many ways my life would have been so much easier if we had gotten together back then. But last night as I was railing about all the wrong turns I've taken, I realized that if that had happened there would be no Sally. No Jason."

"Yeah, that's true."

Heather nodded. ''There's a reason for everything.''

''Even red hair?''

''*Especially* red hair.'' Heather yawned. What an incredible day. She didn't want it to end. But she was so tired. ''Ready to go to bed?''

''You obviously are.''

Before she could say anything, he scooped her—baby and all—into his arms.

''Haven't you had enough of this already?'' she asked, as he carried her to the bedroom.

''I'll never get enough of holding you,'' he promised. On his way out of the room, he flicked the switch and the Christmas lights went out.

The house was dark now, and silent. Heather sank into the softness of their bed, and moments later, felt T.J. join her on the other side. They tucked Teddy between them. He gave a reassuring baby gurgle, and Heather closed her eyes.

She felt an enormous peace settle over her. Deep in her soul she knew that what she had right now, in this bed with her—her husband and her son—were what she'd been moving toward all of her life. She was so glad she'd finally arrived.

# A Full House
## by Nadia Nichols
### (Superromance #1209)

Dr. Annie Crawford's rented an isolated saltwater farm in northern Maine to escape her hectic New York life and to spend time with her troubled teenage daughter. But the two are not alone for long. First comes Nelly—the puppy Annie's ex promised their daughter. Then comes Lily, the elderly owner of the farm who wants nothing more than to return home with her faithful old dog. And finally, Lieutenant Jake Macpherson—the cop who arrested Annie's daughter—shows up with his own little girl. Now Annie's got a full house...and a brand-new family.

*Available in June 2004 wherever Harlequin books are sold.*

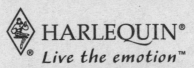

If you enjoyed what you just read,
then we've got an offer you can't resist!

# Take 2 bestselling love stories FREE!

# Plus get a FREE surprise gift!

Clip this page and mail it to Harlequin Reader Service®

**IN U.S.A.**
3010 Walden Ave.
P.O. Box 1867
Buffalo, N.Y. 14240-1867

**IN CANADA**
P.O. Box 609
Fort Erie, Ontario
L2A 5X3

**YES!** Please send me 2 free Harlequin Superromance® novels and my free surprise gift. After receiving them, if I don't wish to receive anymore, I can return the shipping statement marked cancel. If I don't cancel, I will receive 6 brand-new novels every month, before they're available in stores. In the U.S.A., bill me at the bargain price of $4.47 plus 25¢ shipping and handling per book and applicable sales tax, if any*. In Canada, bill me at the bargain price of $4.99 plus 25¢ shipping and handling per book and applicable taxes**. That's the complete price, and a savings of at least 10% off the cover prices—what a great deal! I understand that accepting the 2 free books and gift places me under no obligation ever to buy any books. I can always return a shipment and cancel at any time. Even if I never buy another book from Harlequin, the 2 free books and gift are mine to keep forever.

135 HDN DNT3
336 HDN DNT4

| Name | (PLEASE PRINT) | |
| --- | --- | --- |
| Address | Apt.# | |
| City | State/Prov. | Zip/Postal Code |

\* Terms and prices subject to change without notice. Sales tax applicable in N.Y.
\** Canadian residents will be charged applicable provincial taxes and GST.
  All orders subject to approval. Offer limited to one per household and not valid to current Harlequin Superromance® subscribers.
  ® is a registered trademark of Harlequin Enterprises Limited.

SUP02                                    ©1998 Harlequin Enterprises Limited

# The Man She Married
## by Muriel Jensen
### (Superromance #1208)

Men of
Maple Hill

**Gideon and Prue Hale are still married—but try telling that to Prue. Even though no papers have been signed, as far as Prue's concerned it's over. She can never forgive Gideon's betrayal. Too bad she still misses him….**

*Available June 2004 wherever Harlequin books are sold.*

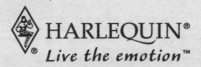

# HARLEQUIN®
## *Live the emotion*™

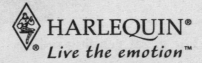